W9-AFJ-348

Copyright © 2022 TNesha Sims

Contents

Hakeem and Serenity:

Convenient love of A Boss

A Novel By
TNesha Sims

Synopsis

Serenity Miller thinks nothing of her living arrangement with her baby's father, Hakeem. Hakeem knows her struggles in life and wants her and his daughter, Naomi, under one roof. Although they are not a couple, they decided to stay together for their daughter's sake. One night, Hakeem asks Serenity about her true feelings for him. When she answers, they ended up in bed together. Serenity is sold on the possibility of them being a family until one day, the female on the other side of Hakeem's room door comes walking out. Serenity knows she can't let jealousy get in the way or deny that she still has feelings for him. She thinks they can possibly work things out, but someone has already claimed Hakeem as their man and makes it known that they'll kill anything and anyone who gets in the way of them being together. Can Serenity prove that she's the only woman for him without dealing with all of the drama, or will she end up dealing with more than she bargains for?

Hakeem does what he has to do to provide for his family at a young age when he finally makes it. After seeing Serenity all over another guy, He is blinded by his rage, although he knows she isn't his woman. But when the empire he built in the streets comes under attack, baby mama drama is the least of his worries. Someone is threatening Hakeem's territory and will stop at nothing to take over everything he worked so hard for. Can Hakeem fight for Serenity's love in the midst of dealing with the madness of the streets, or will his entire life get turned upside down?

Acknowledgment

I want to first thank my family. Your support is greatly appreciated. Thank you to my sister, Terra, who has really motivated me to believe in my dreams and go further. My cousin, Kevin (Terry), you don't know how much more I enjoy writing since you've been reading my books. I can't wait to write more so that I can send them to you. Finally, but most importantly, to my husband, God has placed you in my life for a reason, and I appreciate and cherish everything you do. The way you support me is just amazing. I love you so much. Skee-town, stand up. Special shout out to my cousin Antionette Davis, I love you boo.

Serenity

I woke up to Paw Patrol blasting in the background of my daughter's room. I just knew she was looking to get her little ass whooped. Naomi was only four years old but too smart for her age. I often had to whoop her little ass for her smart-ass mouth. Her teachers always said they had no problem with her at school, but I couldn't believe that because of how she acted at home. I guess she could sense the distance between me and her father. We started out as a couple, but eventually things between us changed. I was tired of him treating me like his child rather than his woman. I guess since he took care of us, he felt that he had to control me. Eventually, we broke up. I had nowhere to go, and I wasn't leaving Naomi. We agreed to live together until I was able to live on my own. My parents had died in a plane that crashed over eight years ago, and I lived with my uncle until I was eighteen. He was never home and didn't care what I did as long as I checked in with him. I left when his girlfriend started stealing the little stuff I did have. I met Hakeem and fell in love with him.

"Naomi, you know better than to have this TV up this loud!" I yelled.

"I couldn't hear because someone is outside cutting the grass," she said with her big brown eyes looking up at me. Naomi looked just like her father. She was light skinned just like him. Her hair was naturally curly and long. She could most definitely do some beauty pageants.

"Girl, you can barely hear them cutting the grass. Don't turn it up like that again, or I'm going to whoop your little butt."

She stared at the TV, but I knew she heard me.

"You hear me?"

"Yes!"

"Yes what?" I asked, ready to whoop her ass.

"Yes ma'am."

"Did your dad feed you?"

"Yes, Mommy. I had oatmeal and toast," she said, smiling. That girl loved oatmeal. Hakeem had her dressed, looking like the doll she was.

I walked away, leaving her to watch her show. I went to shower and brush my teeth. I wore an all-black romper. It was something just to feel comfortable in. I didn't feel like really getting dressed. I walked over to the mirror and noticed my ass was poking out and my stomach was flat. It took me a while after having Naomi to get my body right. I had a cocoa complexion and big eyes as well. My eyes were black and so was my hair. I was five feet four and 150 pounds. I had long curly hair, compliments of my parents, who I missed very much. I had no one but Hakeem, Naomi, and my girl Shayla.

I made it downstairs and knew Hakeem was already gone for the day. He got up super early to only come home late at night. He often popped in when Naomi called asking for him.

I decided to eat a light breakfast and do my homework. I was taking online classes and was in my final week. I couldn't wait to be done. I would have a Bachelor's degree in social work. It was Saturday, and I had to turn in my final paper. Although I'd done it ahead of time, I still wanted to look over everything to be sure. It was easy for me to do my school work because during the week, Naomi would be at school, and Hakeem would be out doing what he did best. He had a nice home with four bedrooms, three bathrooms, and a full basement with a den and his office space. Everything about his home was boss status. I had my own room and so did Naomi. She often asked why her father and I wouldn't sleep in the same bed together, and eventually, we broke the news to her. She cried her little heart out like she really knew what was going on. That's why it was convenient for us to stay together in one house. The way things had been going, I knew it wouldn't last long.

After checking on Naomi, I found her sleeping. I turned her TV off and pulled her door up. I had already cleaned the house the day before, so I wouldn't spend my whole Saturday cleaning. I checked my phone and saw the message Hakeem sent, saying he was going to come get Naomi to take her to have some fun with her grandparents. I rolled my eyes because his mom didn't really like me. He said she didn't have a problem with me, but I couldn't tell. Naomi always came back saying what her grandma said about me. She'd say I needed a job or needed to do something with my life. Neither she nor Hakeem knew I was taking classes online. I guess they just thought I laid around all day and that the house magically cleaned itself.

After getting Naomi ready. I texted her father, letting him know she was ready. It wasn't even five minutes before he walked into the house. His True Religion jeans sagged a little, and I knew he had probably looked all over for his belts. I had rearranged his closet and forgot to tell him where I put them. He wore a chain around his neck, and his royal blue shirt really brought his complexion out. He really needed a touch up on them dreads in his head, but that didn't take away how sexy he was looking.

"What took you so long to text me back, and why it's so damn hot in here?" he asked.

"I didn't have my phone next to me. It was still down here from last night. I don't touch the air, so ask yourself that," I said. Keem always complained about the central air being too cold, so he would turn it off and forget to turn it back on.

"Why you be on the computer so late at night? And have you seen my belts?"

Why you asking all these damn questions, I thought to myself.

"I put them on the back of the door. You just have them lying around your closet, so I rearranged everything for you."

"Damn, let a nigga know next time, or at least put them where I can see them."

I was about to walk away when he called after me. I turned around to show how irritated I was with him already.

"Drop the attitude. I asked you two questions, but you only gave me one answer."

"Who the fuck I look like, Naomi?" I asked.

"I just got here, and you going at it already!" he raised his voice at me.

"Your daughter is ready," I said, walking away.

"I hope you packed enough stuff. She's spending the night with my moms."

"Did you ask me if she could spend the night?"

"I don't have to."

He walked away, and I wanted to curse him so bad, but I decided to just go and call my girl Shayla.

Hakeem

"Baby, when can I spend the night at your house?" Rika asked me. Rika was my lil' baby. Although I hadn't made shit official yet, niggas knew she was off limits. Her fat ass and big breast had me at hello. She was dark skinned and sexy as fuck. I had been seeing her for almost a year. I just told her about my daughter, but I didn't mention she stayed with me, along with her mother. No one would believe my baby mama was staying with me and that I wasn't fucking her. Truth was, we hadn't fucked in over two years. When we broke up, I knew she didn't have a place to go. I was all she had, and I wasn't going to do the mother of my child like that. I never brought females to my crib, and she never brought niggas over. In fact, she wasn't even allowed to talk to other niggas while I was caring for her. I knew it was wrong, but it was only right. Serenity was fine as fuck, and I often got tempted to fuck her, but I knew she would reject a nigga anyway. We agreed to end our relationship. At first, I wanted to try again, but I got used to the convenience of being around my daughter and baby mama.

I was light skinned with dimples. I had dreads, which I often thought about cutting off. My hazel eyes always had bitches dropping them panties. I was about six feet three. I was built and had tats all over my body. My daughter looked just like me, only she had big brown eyes. She had her mama's big eyes. Although I wasn't with Serenity, I cared for her and wanted her to eventually be happy in life. I wouldn't say I wanted it to be with another nigga but for her to get her own everything. She drove one of my cars and used my black card. Oh, yes! At the age of 27 a nigga was getting it. Living in San Antonio, Texas, I was the man. I didn't expect to take over my homeboy Dex's empire, but when he retired and wanted to get out and handed it down to me, I took that shit and ran with it. He often popped in when I needed him, but that was years ago.

"Keem?" Rika called out to me.

"Look, I have to tell you something else about my baby mama."

"Shit, is she the crazy type? Are y'all still fucking around?"

"Nah, she's cool, but she's living with me for the time being."

"What?"

"It ain't even like that. We don't even sleep in the same room. We're doing it for our daughter. Eventually, when she gets on her feet, she'll move out."

"Hakeem, what the fuck? I know you, and I know you could get her a place for her and your daughter. Why does she have to live there?"

"Because of our daughter."

"You know what? I'm not even tripping. If you introduce us and I check shit out for myself, I'll believe you."

"So bringing you to my crib would make it believable?"

"Yep, and let me spend the night."

"Look. Serenity and I have this rule about not bringing people to the house just out of respect of one another, but I'll introduce you to my daughter, and if her mother's there, I'll introduce y'all."

"When?"

"I'll let you know, shorty."

"Yeah, okay."

"I have to get going though. I'm taking my daughter some-where. I'll holla at you later, baby."

I got off the couch and gave her a stack to make her happy for the time being. I knew she didn't need that shit, but she never complained when I dropped bread on her.

I had just pulled up to my crib when I got the text from Serenity saying that our daughter was ready. I had been waiting for her response for over four hours. I walked in the house to her ass poking through the outfit she had on. Not being with her in two years, I guess I was over the attraction for her.

After going back and forth with Serenity, I finally walked off to get my daughter. She always had an attitude. and I could never understand why. Every decision I made, she didn't agree with, but I paid her ass no mind.

As soon as I got into my princess's room, she leapt from her bed and ran over to hug me.

"Daddy!" she yelled out.

"Hey, princess. What have you been doing all day?"

"Watching TV and dealing with the mean lady," she said.

"What I tell you about repeating what Daddy says?" I said. I often referred to Serenity as the mean lady.

"Sorry," she said, looking down.

"Aww, it's okay, baby. Daddy is not mad," I said, tickling her. I grabbed her bags and headed downstairs.

"Bye, Mommy," Naomi said.

"Umm, little girl, is that all I get?"

I walked Naomi over to her mom because I didn't want to put her down only to have to pick her back up. She kissed her mom's lips and looked at me and kissed my cheek.

"Kiss for Mommy and Daddy. Now Daddy, can you kiss

Mommy? You never kiss Mommy," she said, pouting. I didn't know what had gotten into her. She knew what was going on with us, so for her to say that was crazy to me.

"Naomi, you know why I don't kiss Mommy."

"No, Daddy. I don't."

I looked at Serenity, and she stared at me. I didn't know what to say.

"We have to go, princess. Your granny is waiting for you."

I walked away and headed for the door. Serenity walked us outside and waved us off. In the car, I played my music, and Naomi all of the sudden started yelling out to me.

"What, baby? What?" I asked, turning the music down.

"Do you love Mommy?"

"Yes, I do."

"Why didn't you kiss her?"

"Because I don't want to kiss Mommy. Your mom and I are only friends now. We told you this."

"I want you and Mommy to be like Ken."

"Ken? Who the hell is Ken?"

"Daddy, you said bad word."

"Naomi, who is Ken?"

"You know... Ken and Barbie."

She talking about a damn doll. I thought for a moment that it was someone her mother had brought around her.

"Because we can't. Now be quiet before I tell grandma not to give you any cookies when we get to her house."

I turned the music back up, looking at her pouting face. Her lil' grown ass was too much for me.

I walked into my parents' crib, and my mom met us at the

door. Naomi jumped into her arms and hugged her.

"Are you still going to the park with us?" my mom asked.

"I was, but I'm getting tired. I been working all day."

"The streets isn't what you call working, Hakeem."

"Not in front of the B.A.B.Y, Mom," I said, spelling it out.

"I'm not a baby," Naomi said.

"You can't hide nothing from this child. I tell ya, she's been here before."

I laughed and walked into the living room. My pops sat on the couch, eating some type of pie. Coli was my stepfather, but he'd been in my life since I was about two years old. My father left my mother before I was born. My mother, Denise, cared for me and did a damn good job. That's why I put her and my father in that big ass house. They didn't agree with my life style, but they respected it.

After chatting with him, Naomi finally ran and jumped into his lap. I left them alone and knew she would get whatever she wanted from them the time I hit the door.

"Aight, Mom. I'm going to head out."

"Serenity hasn't found a job yet?" she asked.

"No. I don't know if she's even looking. I'm not worried about it, so why are you?"

"You better watch that tongue, Hakeem."

"I'm just saying, what we have right now is straight."

"Whatever, boy. You think it's going to be a good idea bringing Rika over there while Serenity is living there?"

"Rika and I will have that understanding when the time comes."

"You're still in love with Serenity. Otherwise, that living arrangement wouldn't even exist."

"I have to go, Mom."

I left because I didn't want to get into that conversation with my mother.

I looked at my phone and read Serenity's text she had sent me.

Serenity: *I'm headed over Shayla's in a bit*

Me: *For what?*

Serenity: *?*

Me: *Nvm... do you, I hope you locked up.*

Serenity: *Duh, isn't that what people do when they leave their home.*

Me: *You got a home?*

Serenity: *Don't worry, Hakeem. I'll be out your home soon.*

I felt bad when I sent that text, but I knew it was too late. Reading that she would be gone soon was something new to me. I needed to sit down and talk with her.

I decided to go over my boy's crib. It was Friday, and I needed to get loose.

Serenity

"**G**irl, why haven't you found a job yet? I can't believe you dealing with Keem and his shit," Shayla said.

"I admit that it's getting to be too much. I'm tired of seeing his face every day."

"Maybe if you fuck his face, you wouldn't."

"Shay, stop it. I'm not even attracted to him anymore."

"Who you think you talking to? I'm your best friend, and I know you still love him."

"I really don't."

"Then why are you still single? It's been what, two years now?"

"Hakeem and I have rules, and dating while living under his roof is one."

"Wait, wait, wait. So because you're living with him, you can't date, but that nigga slanging dick all over the state of Texas?"

"I know it seems crazy, but I don't mind obeying his rules. I'll be graduating soon, and hopefully I'll find a good internship and get the experience I need. I do plan to apply at your job. Are you guys hiring?" I asked.

"We are for the back room. We need someone to do inventory in our database every week, just making sure the data matches with the data on paper. It pays good to be what it is, and I think they only want a high school diploma."

"Bitch, why didn't you tell me about it before?"

"You never expressed interest in working until now," she said in a matter-of-fact tone.

"I guess you're right."

"It's all good, friend. I'm proud of you. We should go out tonight. You already said Naomi is with her grandma."

"Where, first?"

"Don't do me like that. It'll be fun."

"You know I'm not twenty-one yet, so don't have me going places to only get turned around."

"Girl, bye. That would never happen being with me, and your twenty-first birthday around the corner. What you want to do?"

"I don't know. I don't even have money to do anything, and it's not around the corner. It's in a few months"

"That's right around the corner, and don't you have Keem's black card?"

"Yes, that's mainly for shit around the house and for Naomi."

"I'm going to have to school you, boo. Let's go to the mall and find something for tonight, and I'll do your hair."

I didn't argue with Shayla. When she wanted something, she got on my nerves until I gave in.

We walked around the mall and shopped. Shayla bought a dress for me that I planned on not wearing. I wasn't even in the mood to go out.

"I'll drive, boo, because I know Hakeem will use that as an excuse for you to come home. Nigga be like *hey, Serenity. I need the Bentley. Come switch cars with me*. Like, who the hell going to leave from the club and come all the way back? Your baby daddy be knowing what the hell he be doing."

"Whatever, Shay, but hurry up so that I can grab my stuff. I'm staying at your house tonight."

She followed me to Hakeem's, and I parked his car and ran inside to get my things. I locked up and jumped into her car.

"Do not text that man your every move," she said as I was about to text Hakeem.

"I'm just letting him know I won't be home."

She grabbed my phone, and I laughed. I must say that she was really trying to school a bitch.

We walked inside the club, and I could smell the cigarettes. I hated that smell. We sat at the bar, and Shayla ordered us drinks. We didn't even get asked for our IDs, and I was thankful.

"What's this?" I asked as she handed me the drink.

"Sex on the beach, something you need."

She laughed.

"Bitch, shut up."

We sat at the bar dancing in our seats. Two dudes walked up and talked to Shayla. Then, she turned and pointed at me.

"This my girl Serenity. Serenity, this Dre and Darnell.

"Sup, sexy?" the Darnell dude said to me. Shayla got up and walked away. Darnell sat in her place.

This bitch set me up, I thought to myself.

"That name is beautiful," Darnell spoke.

"Thanks," I said, being short. He was cute, but I didn't like being set up.

"So Shay told me that you're single and looking to date."

Shay? How long has she known these niggas? Only people we're close to call her that.

"She was mistaken. I'm not really looking to date right now. I'm focused on school."

"Oh yeah? What are you majoring in?"

"Social work," I said proudly.

"Okay, that's what's up. 'Miss Go Getter' I see."

To hear him say that brought a smile to my face. No one had ever said that to me. No one really knew I was in school either, besides Shayla.

"Thanks."

"So, can I call you sometimes?" he asked.

Girl, give this man your number. He is sexy as fuck, and he smells good. My thoughts were too loud for me to even say no. I pulled my phone out and told him to give me his as well.

"I'm going to call you when I get home. It's too loud in here to be trying to get to know someone," he said.

"Okay," I said in his ear. His boy Dre ran over and said my girl was on her way to jail.

"What?" I said, jumping from my seat.

"They towed her car, and she snapped on the police. She really didn't do shit wrong, but they told her if she didn't get back that they were taking her to jail. Y'all know how them fuckers are."

I ran outside to see what was going on. On my way out, I bumped into someone and dropped my phone.

"Damn. My bad, cutie," he said. I knew that voice from anywhere. I grabbed my phone from the ground and looked up at Hakeem.

"Serenity?" he asked, like he couldn't believe it was me.

"I... I got to check on Shay." I made it all the way out, and sure enough, right in front of the club, the police had Shay in the back seat. I looked at her, but she wasn't looking at me. They pulled off, and I turned to look at Dre and Darnell. I didn't notice Hakeem standing behind them.

"Dre, what the fuck happened?" I snapped.

"We came out here to smoke, and she noticed her car getting towed."

"I told her not to park there," I said.

"You need a ride home, lil' mama. I got you," Darnell said. I don't know why I felt like I was being disrespectful to Hakeem when we weren't even together.

"I… umm."

"Nah, she straight," Hakeem spoke. They turned around and looked at him. Dre gave him some dap and introduced Darnell to Hakeem. I was standing there looking stupid, not knowing what to say.

"Damn, so this you?" Darnell asked Hakeem.

"Nah, but she's off limits though."

Off limits? Bitch, who the fuck is you, I thought to myself.

"Why? Is she your sister?" he asked. I folded my arms across my chest, waiting for the comment to make Hakeem's ass look fucking crazy.

"That's my baby mama."

"I'll respect that, so I guess you'll make sure she gets home, right?" Darnell asked.

"Yeah, I will," Hakeem said. They walked away, and I stared at Hakeem like I wanted to kill him.

"You can't be serious," I said.

"As a heart attack. Now let's go."

"I don't have to do shit you say. You ain't my man. You're just Naomi's father. That's it."

"That's it? Bitch, who the fuck taking care of your trifling ass?"

I couldn't believe he had said that shit to me and was calling me out my name. Enough was enough. I was so tired of him telling the world what he did for me. I called an Uber and stood on the curb. He mumbled something, but I was so heated that I didn't even hear him.

"Keem? What are you doing?" some chick asked, walking up to him. I looked their way and wanted to see what his next move would be.

"I'm trying to make sure Serenity gets home safe."

"Your baby mama?" she asked. She knew too much for me, and I wanted to know exactly who she was.

"Look, I'll explain later."

Explain what? Who is this bitch, I thought to myself. She walked over to me and stood toe to toe with me as she looked me up and down. All I knew was Hakeem better had gotten her big forehead ass before I dog walked her ass. He knew I didn't play that shit.

"So, you're the one leeching off my man."

"Rika, shut the fuck up. Go sit in my ride. I'll be there in a minute," he said, pulling her away from me. I had no words because if she said anything else, he would be picking her up off the ground. She walked away, still talking shit to him. I rolled my eyes at him, and he looked at me like he really felt some type of way.

"Look. My girl pissed off right now, so I need to handle that. I can still give you a ride."

"Hakeem, get the fuck away from me."

I walked off. My Uber had finally pulled up, and I went to Shay's house. I had her keys in my purse. She had asked me to hold them because she didn't want to bring her purse in. Inside Shay's house, I wondered what it was I could do. She hadn't called yet, and I was worried. I called to see if she had gotten booked in, and they told me she was released already.

Why the fuck didn't she call me?

I called her phone, and it was dead. I assumed that's why she hadn't called. The doorbell rang, and I ran to see if it was her. Sure enough, it was. I looked at the car that dropped her off and knew it was Hakeem's friend, Rashad.

"Bitch, was that Rashad?" I asked, letting her in.

"Girl, yes. I called him to bail me out. You know that's my baby. When he stops being a hoe, we gon' be together."

"Bitch, you too much. I'm happy you're out though."

"So what happened between you and Darnell?" she asked. We sat on the couch, and I told her everything. She got pissed when I told her about Hakeem and his bitch, Rika.

"His ass lucky I was already in jail," she said. I laughed and got up to take a shower. I was still pissed off, but I knew I just needed to get my shit together and move out.

Lying in the bed with Shay, I thought about my future. Besides Hakeem and our daughter, she was all I had. I hated feeling like I had to depend on Hakeem. He was really showing his true colors.

"You okay, Serenity?" she asked.

"Yeah, just thinking about my future. I just want to make it and not depend on Hakeem for shit."

"You can stay here, you and my goddaughter."

"You already know he ain't going for that."

"Well, when you start working, you can get a place. I'll cosign for you. I'm tired of him having so much power over you."

"Aww, thanks, Shay. I haven't established any credit yet, so that would be awesome."

"Girl, you know I got you, and are you going to call Darnell?"

"I don't know. Being that he knows Hakeem, it don't even feel right."

"Are they boys? You said Dre introduced them, and fuck Keem's feelings."

Hakeem

"**S**o that bitch all in the club like she got money to be spending?" Rika asked.

"Aye, chill out," I told her.

"What? I'm just saying. Why she ain't using that energy to find a job? That just shows what type of mother she is."

"Man, what the fuck I say!" I yelled. Despite what others may think, Serenity was a damn good mother to our daughter. That's why Naomi was so smart.

"Oh, so you mad? Fuck that bitch. You better put that hoe out, or we're done."

"I'm not going to put Naomi's mother out. What type of father would I be?"

"One that is going to be single."

"Look… ain't shit going on with me and Serenity. I'm supposed to make sure my child's mother gets home safe."

"Yeah, the home you're sharing? If I tell my friends this shit, they would laugh at my ass."

"That's your fucking problem. You're too worried about what other people think!"

I pulled up to her house. She got out and slammed my door. She knew I didn't play that shit. I didn't even wait until she got in the house before I pulled off.

My phone rang, and it was her.

"What, Rika?"

"That's how I know you're still fucking her. You're so worried about her getting home safe, but you couldn't even wait until I got in the house before you pulled off."

She hung up, and I didn't even call her ass back. I got home and saw my Bentley, so I knew Serenity was there. I was going apologize for saying that shit to her outside the club. I walked in and had to turn my alarm off. I knew I had turned it on before I left, and I remembered that the Bentley was there when I came home to change clothes. I had assumed she drove it to Shay's house.

Damn, she ain't even here. Where the fuck she at, I thought to myself. I called her, but it went straight to voicemail. She knew better. What if our daughter was sick? I called and called, and it still went to the voicemail. I called her on my trap phone. The only people that had that number were my boy Rashad and a few of my soldiers in my crew.

"Hello?" she answered.

"So you sending my shit to voicemail on purpose?" I snapped.

"Hakeem, what the fuck do you want?"

"Where you at?"

"None of your fucking business."

"It is my business."

"See, that's where this shit gets crazy at. I'm not your girl, so you shouldn't be worried about me. I'm grown as hell and don't need to check in with you about my whereabouts."

"I think we need to talk."

"Ain't shit to talk about. If it's not about Naomi, we shouldn't even be talking."

"So that's how you gon' play me?" I asked.

"Don't make me block this number too," she said and hung up. I didn't even bother calling her back.

∞∞∞

It was the next morning, and my head was banging. I didn't sleep well, and I usually slept like a baby. I got up, showered, and brushed and flossed my teeth. I checked the mail, only to find a package sitting on my steps. It had Serenity's name on it, but I still opened it.

Congratulations on your upcoming graduation. Please read the enclosed information about the ceremony and do's and don'ts for the occasion.

I read over the rest and felt confused. It stated her online courses were almost finished and that she would be graduating soon. I grabbed her laptop and turned it on. I went to her history. Sure enough, it showed Blackboard courses, but it showed an error page because I needed to sign in. *Damn when did she start taking online classes? Is that why she said something about her being gone soon?*

I decided to go get Naomi so that we could spend our Saturday together. Soon as she got into the car, she talked about the fun she had.

"It's hot back here, Daddy," she said. I turned the AC on and rolled the windows up. It was March, and it was hot as hell. We got home, and Naomi took off running like she always did. Not even two minutes later, she ran back looking at me.

"What?"

"Where is Mommy," she asked.

"I don't know."

"You lost my mommy!" she yelled.

"Watch who you're talking to, and no, she left."

"Left where?"

"Naomi, go in your room before I whoop you."

"But you never whoop me," she said, starting to cry. *She too damn spoiled,* I thought to myself.

"Daddy sorry. Just go watch a movie until it's time to go for ice cream later, okay?"

"Okay," she said, taking off. I looked at my phone and saw a missed call from Rika. I didn't feel like dealing with her shit today.

Naomi and I were driving down the street when she asked if she could call her mama. I called Serenity from my trap phone, put it on speaker, and gave it to Naomi.

"Why the fuck are you calling me!"

"Mommy, that's a naughty word."

"Hey, baby. I'm sorry. I thought you were your dad calling."

"Mommy, when are you coming home. I miss you."

"Aww, baby, I'll be there in a bit."

"Where are you?" Naomi asked.

"At your god mommy's house."

"Can I come see Shay? Mama, please?"

"No, not today, baby."

Naomi got quiet, and that meant her feelings were hurt.

"Of course you can come see your favorite god mom," Shay said, getting on the phone. I headed toward that direction. Naomi always did what I wanted without me even telling her. I wanted her to say everything she said to Serenity. We pulled up to Shay's house, and I let Naomi ring the doorbell. Shay opened the door and picked Naomi up, hugging her. She mugged me, and I laughed. That little mug wasn't scaring anybody. Serenity appeared in the doorway looking beautiful. Her hair was straight and hanging down. It was one of the styles I used to love on her.

"Mommy, Daddy is taking me to get ice cream. Can you come too?"

Serenity looked at me, and I smiled. I knew she couldn't tell the princess no, even if she wanted to.

"I guess, but I'm sitting in the back with you."

Serenity headed back in the house and gathered her things. Shay walked over to me and stood before me.

"You ain't shit, Keem."

"That's for us, sis?"

"Sis? You lost that privilege when you and Serenity broke up."

"So what about Rashad? Don't that still make us bro and sis?"

"Leave my house, before I hurt you."

I laughed and walked around to my car to get in.

"Mommy, Daddy wanted to whoop me," Naomi said as I drove to get her ice cream.

"Stop telling a story," I said to them in the back seat. Serenity didn't say anything.

We made it to the park, and I bought ice cream for Naomi. I offered to get Serenity some, but she declined. After Naomi finished her ice cream, she went to play as we sat on the benches watching her.

"Yo, my fault about the shit I said at the club. I know if you could have your own shit that you would. I don't know why I said that. I guess I felt some type of way," I confessed. I couldn't believe I had even told her that. She didn't respond, and I knew she was in deep thought.

"So, when were you going to tell me that you were taking online classes?"

That got her attention.

"I didn't think it was necessary for you to know."

"Why wouldn't I want to know about that?"

"Look, it's no big deal.

"It's a real big deal."

She got up and walked away, and I just didn't understand how we got to the place we were in. Naomi walked over, saying she wanted to go home. I laughed because she was just too damn demanding.

My phone vibrated, and it was Rika. I answered because I was starting to miss her crazy ass.

"Yeah."

"Hey, are you busy?" she asked.

"Kind of. I just left from taking Naomi to the park. Why? What's up?"

"I think we need to talk."

"When I drop Naomi off, I'll be there."

"Mommy, Mommy, look," Naomi said.

"What number is that?" Serenity asked her.

"It's the number five," Naomi said. I smiled because Naomi always liked showing her mother that she knew her numbers.

"Is your baby mama with you?" Rika asked.

"Yeah."

Silence.

"Hello!" I said, looking at the phone.

"I'm here."

"I'll be there in a little bit," I said. She hung up, and I knew she was going to lose that nice attitude that she had called with. Once we got home, Serenity bathed Naomi and put her to bed. She walked out of her room, and we bumped into each other.

"My fault," I said, looking down at her. She was beautiful and deserved so much more. *Maybe I didn't try hard enough to make things work between us.* I hated when I started those crazy thoughts.

"Can you move?" she asked.

"Oh, damn," I said, moving out her way.

When she walked by, I stared at her ass. She had been working out, and it was paying off.

Serenity

I had just walked across the stage to get my degree. Naomi, Shay, Hakeem, Rashad, and Hakeem's parents all cheered me on. I had invited my uncle, and he declined to come. I knew it was because of his girlfriend. I was so proud of myself, and I started my internship at the prison the following week. I was only working three days a week at the company Shay worked for, but it was income coming in.

"I'm so proud of you, girl," Shay said, hugging me. I hugged her back, and then Naomi ran over to me. I scooped her up and kissed her. She was my motivation to keep going. Rashad hugged me next and told me congratulations.

"Congratulations! I still can't believe you guys didn't tell me you were in school," Denise said. *For what? You're too busy downing me to listen anyway.* I forced a smile at her and hugged her. I did the same with Hakeem's father.

"Congrats," Hakeem said, hugging me. We hadn't hugged in years. It felt weird in a way. After dinner at the restaurant, we headed home. Shay wanted to go out for drinks, but of course Hakeem said he had business to attend to. Since his parents had already left, I wasn't going to call them up to ask if they could baby sit. I had never called and asked them before. It was always Hakeem who asked. That was the only time I usually left the house to hang out anyway.

"Maybe tomorrow," I told Shay.

Naomi was in bed sleeping peacefully. I turned her TV off and shut her door half way. Since Hakeem was out, I decided to take a bath in his bathroom. His tub was the biggest, and I often used it when he was gone.

I blew out the candle I had lit and got out the tub. Once I dressed, I would be back to clean it out. I wrapped the big towel around me and walked out the bathroom. I came face to face with Hakeem. Well, we weren't really face to face, because he was taller.

"Sup?" he asked.

"Oh, sorry. I used your bathroom. I'll clean it after I get dressed."

"Serenity, it's cool. I know you use it often. I'm not tripping.

He was being too nice for me. He moved, and I started to walk away.

"Do you think about trying again sometimes?" he asked. I turned around, not understanding the question.

"Trying what?" I asked.

"Trying with me again," he said, leaning against the door frame.

"What you mean?" I didn't want to answer the question not knowing what he was talking about.

"Us, Serenity."

"Us what?"

"Being together."

"Sometimes," I confessed. He looked down at me and walked over to me. I started walking backwards because of the look in his eyes. I hadn't seen that look in two years.

He pulled the towel from my body, and a lump formed in my throat. I didn't understand why he was doing what he was doing. I stood naked before him. I wasn't bothered, because my body was flawless. Then, he kissed me, and I kissed him back. He pulled me toward his customized king size bed. He laid me down and spread my legs. Kissing my thighs, I closed my eyes because he stared up at me. I felt what we were doing was wrong, but the feeling was right.

"Ahh… right there, Hakeem," I said as he sucked and slurped. I hadn't had that feeling for so long. I had masturbated, but that was different. He pulled his dick out and entered me, and it was a bit uncomfortable for a minute, but eventually, it started to feel good.

"This pussy still the way I left it," he said, beating my pussy up. I couldn't respond because I was too busy cummin'.

"You miss this dick, don't you?" he asked.

"Yes, I do."

I had to admit I did. After Hakeem fucked me so good, I laid there, but the feeling I felt was confusing. I knew we shouldn't have crossed those lines, but we did. He had been drinking. I could taste the liquor when he kissed me. I got up and walked to my room. I washed up and checked on Naomi.

Lying in bed, I couldn't believe what had happened between me and Hakeem. *Why did he ask if I thought about trying with him again? Why did my dumb ass tell him sometimes I did think about him? I shouldn't have told him that,* I thought to myself.

I couldn't sleep, because the thoughts I had about my baby daddy consumed my mind. I didn't know what having sex meant for us. After all those years, I still loved him, but I tried my best to hide those feelings from him and myself.

It was morning when I woke up. I didn't know what time

I had actually fallen asleep, but I was glad I finally did. I took care of my personal hygiene and headed to my baby's room. She wasn't there, so I knew she was up with her father. I looked around her room. Her bed was made, and everything was in its place. I walked downstairs and found them eating in the kitchen.

I kissed Naomi on the check, and she perked her lips up, screaming *good morning, Mommy*. I poured up some orange juice, ignoring Hakeem. I could feel his eyes on me.

"Good moaning," he said. I knew he was fucking with me. Why else would he say that shit? I ignored him, but he called my name.

"Yeah."

I turned around.

"You can't speak?" he asked.

"Hey."

I didn't know what to say. All I knew was that we'd had sex when we shouldn't have.

"You got plans for Naomi today? My moms wants to take her with her for the weekend."

And leave me alone with you? I think not, I thought to myself.

"I wanted to take her to the parade."

"My mom wants to take her to it."

"Okay," I said. I walked away and headed back to my room. I made my bed and headed to Naomi's room to get her things packed for her weekend away.

Hakeem and Naomi left, and I had cleaned the whole house. I planned to get up with Shay and enjoy the weekend with her. I wanted to be gone before Hakeem came back.

Hakeem

I had just dropped Naomi off to my mom's for the weekend, and I was going to head over to Rika's crib. I knew it seemed foul that I had fucked Serenity while still with Rika, but Rika had pissed me the fuck off. She called in the morning, asking if we could talk and told me she just felt like I put Serenity before her and that she really loved me. I couldn't say I didn't understand her feelings, because the situation between my baby mama and I was different.

"Sup, sexy," I said, walking into Rika's crib.

"Keem, I really love you, and I was just hurt because it seems like I'll always be last in your life. I know Naomi comes first, and I understand that, but your baby mama shouldn't come before me."

"Baby, you don't have anything to worry about. It's not like that between us."

"Can I spend the night with you tonight? You said Naomi is gone for the weekend, right?"

"Yeah, she is. I'll just stay here," I told her. I knew what she was thinking, but I had fucked up and slept with Serenity. That would be too much to bring Rika around.

"Whatever."

"Come let me take care of you," I said to her. I pulled her clothes off and showed her how much I cared for her.

"Your dick can't always fix everything," she said, enjoying my kisses.

"Shut up," I told her. After making up with Rika, I left to handle business. I met up with Rashad at the hub. It was a spot where we talked business. We just came up with that name.

"Sup, nigga?" I asked him.

"Ain't shit, fool. Just got done hollering at Shayla."

"What's up with y'all?"

"She think a nigga a hoe, so she won't fuck with me like that, but she'll let me fuck her back out though."

"Your ass is a hoe, nigga," I said, laughing.

"Man, whatever. That's all me though."

"Yeah, okay."

"Fuck you coming from?" he asked.

"Rika's house."

He didn't say shit to that, because Rashad couldn't stand Rika. He said she was sneaky. I paid it no mind, because I really liked her, and she had never shown signs of being disloyal.

"I fucked Serenity last night."

Rashad and I told each other everything, so he was used to me blurting out shit.

"Nigga, what?"

"Man, I got home, and she was coming out of my bathroom. She only had a towel wrapped around her. She smelled so good too. I asked her if she ever thought about trying it with me again, and she said yeah. I was shocked that she said that, but one thing lead to another, and yeah. We fucked."

"You ain't right, bruh, talking about me. You got Rika and Serenity. I like your style."

"It ain't even like that. I think Serenity just needed to get fucked. She didn't show any emotions this morning."

"I don't know. That's dangerous. You had a good thing going on. Why fuck it up? Either be with Serenity, who I think is a better woman for you, or be with that hoe Rika."

"Man, chill on Rika. She's straight. I actually like her."

"But you're still in love with Serenity."

I thought about what he said and changed the subject. That's not why I called to meet up with him.

"Anyway, I got them niggas lined up, waiting for that weight. Only problem is, I can't make that drop. My daughter has this lil' father-daughter function at her school, so I need you and one of the soldiers to go."

"I got you, nigga, but what you on tonight? You trying to go to that spring bash at Club 60 tonight?"

"Hell yeah. We can do that. Naomi with my moms for the weekend, so I'm partying all weekend."

"Nigga, when she ain't with your moms, you still party all weekend."

He just had to remind me.

"Whatever. It's hot as hell though out here. You rolling with me later, or you solo?"

"I don't know yet. Your ass stay in some shit with that Rika bitch. You know her ass gon' be all up in there."

"Nah, I told that ass to stay at home tonight. She knows better."

"I ain't tryin' to be stranded, nigga, fucking with you."

"You gon' be straight. I'll come scoop ya ass later."

I jumped in my ride and headed home. When I got there, Serenity wasn't even there. I shook my head because I knew she was gon' leave once Naomi went to my mom's. I decided I needed some shoes, so I headed to the mall to cop a few pair.

I grabbed Naomi and Serenity the new Jordan's that had come out. It wasn't shit though. I did that shit all the time. Every time I bought myself something, I copped them something too.

"Hey, Hakeem," some chick said, walking by. I spoke and kept it to moving. Don't get me wrong. Rika wasn't the only chick I was fucking. She was just the main one, the only one I was caught seen with in the streets. Everyone else called her my girl, but I never officially asked her that. Being that we were always together, I guess she was.

My moms called me and said Naomi was ready to come home. I stopped by there because I knew what it was. Naomi was spoiled, and when she didn't get her way, she would pull a fast one over you.

"Sup, ma?" I asked my mother, walking in her house.

"Nothing. That child of yours is too grown. She got that mouth from her mother."

"Ma, how can you even say that? Serenity is always respectful when she's around you."

"Do you notice that when someone says anything about that girl, you defend her?"

"Ma, you tripping. Where Naomi at?"

We walked to the back, and she was sitting on the couch watching TV. My mom said she told her to go to bed, but she asked to go home.

"Naomi," I called out to her.

"Daddy!"

She jumped into my arms and hugged me. I picked her up and asked what the problem was.

"I want to go home."

"Why... because granny told you to go to bed? If you come home, you're going to bed also, so you might as well stay here.

Granny taking you somewhere fun tomorrow, but if you keep acting up, you ain't going nowhere, and I'm taking your toys away for a week. You know when granny says go to bed, you have to listen to what she says."

Now you would think me saying that would make her just say *okay Daddy*, but no. She wanted to cry like I had cursed her out or something. Serenity told me I had her spoiled, but I didn't know it was that bad.

"Naomi, why are you crying? I'm just telling you what will happen if you don't listen to your grandma. Go to bed, and I'll take you to that cupcake shop next weekend, but you have to be good and listen."

"Okay, Daddy," she said. Tears were still coming down her face, and I had to chuckle. She was too much for me at times.

"Aight, ma. I'm out. Stop letting her get away with stuff. It's okay to be stern with her."

"Boy, get out my house, and where you going?"

"Out with Rashad."

"Where is Serenity?"

"I don't know. I don't keep tabs on her."

"Yeah, whatever. Well, call me tomorrow, and be safe out there."

Shayla

"**G**irl, why Rashad just called and asked if we wanted to go to that spring bash tonight?"

"What you tell him?" Serenity asked.

"I told him we might but just not together."

"You always do the most. I'm not trying to see Keem tonight."

"Why? What's going on?"

I didn't know what was going on with my girl. I knew she said she was down to go out, but now it seemed like she was backing out on me.

"I slept with him."

"With who?" I asked.

"Hakeem, my baby daddy. I fucked up. He caught me slipping."

"So he caught you slipping and what… eased up inside of your pussy? What the hell you mean *he caught you slipping*?"

"Bitch, shut up, but I was coming out of his bathroom, and he walked in. I apologized for using his bathroom, and he said it was cool. I tried to walk away, and he asked did I ever think about trying again with him, you know, to be together? My dumb ass said yeah. Next thing I know, he was fucking me so good. Do you know how long it's been?"

"Damn, so he had you like that?" I asked.

"I shouldn't have let that happen though. Things are going to get complicated, and I know it's going to affect our relationship now. I just can't deal with that."

"Can you just admit that you are still in love with him?"

"It doesn't matter, but he has a girl. Well, I think he does. I don't know."

"Bitch, he can't be with that hoe if he's back trying to fuck with you."

"Okay, let's just say I do still love him. We didn't work the first time, so what will be different now?"

"You cummin' every night on his dick."

"See, I can't even talk to you. Is you going to do my hair or not?"

"Chick, don't rush me."

I got the flat irons ready and started flat ironing her hair. We talked about her goals, where she wanted to be in five years, and of course Naomi.

I worked for an advertising firm that helped people build their brand and other companies build theirs. It was a great company, and I made decent money. I wanted to get the big gigs like helping celebrities build their brand or get endorsement deals, but the only thing my manager gave me was those shitty companies that wanted someone to slave by building their brand, only for them to treat their customers like shit and ruin their own reputation.

"Shay! Bitch, you just burnt my neck. What the hell is you thinking about?" she asked me.

"My fault, but I really like Rashad. I just know what type of dude he is, and I'm not trying to get my heart broken. I will fuck him and a bitch up. I can't be out here fighting the whole state of Texas over his ass."

"Maybe if you give him the chance, he will show you another side."

"Serenity, remember I did that, and the nigga was fucking two bitches at the same time. Even if we weren't together, that just shows he's a hoe."

"Okay, fuck Rashad and Keem. We're going to have a good time tonight. I'm tired of turning niggas down to spare Keem's feelings. It's time for me to get a man of my own, and I advise you to do the same."

My bitch, I thought to myself.

"Yes, let me get this hair together because we gon' slay to the gods tonight."

I curled Serenity's hair, and she showered and got dressed. I bumped my bob that I rocked and got myself ready as well. It was already close to 11:00 p.m.

We pulled up and parked through valet because I wasn't about to walk up the street in some heels. My girl and I stepped out, and heads started turning right away. I wore a royal blue fitted dress with a pair of nude heels. It complemented my high yellow skin tone. My light brown eyes and one dimple drove those niggas wild. The ass and flat stomach was only a bonus if you asked me because my face alone shut bitches down. There was one nigga in particular that I wanted to bag, but he wasn't ready for a woman like me. Serenity wore a sexy mesh see-through bodycon jumpsuit. I swear she was just as bad as I was.

"Damn, they bad as fuck!" someone yelled out. We paid them no mind. We walked to the VIP section, and the guy asked for our names.

"We didn't buy a section, but we ain't trying to wait in no line either," I told him. I knew Serenity was getting nervous, being that she wasn't twenty-one yet, but I just wanted to mess with her ass.

"I need to see some I.D first."

I looked at Serenity, and she looked scared. I burst out laughing and so did Nut. Nut was the bouncer, and he always let me do my thing.

"I'm just playing with you, girl. Nut got us."

She rolled her eyes, and we walked in. They escorted us to a small section in VIP. Even though we didn't get a VIP section, Nut made sure they took care of us.

"Bitch, you play to damn much!" Serenity yelled.

"I had to, friend, but what you drinking on?"

"Get that drink you got me a while ago at the other club!" she yelled back.

"Aight."

I waited for the waitress to bring her ass over to us and placed our orders. I looked around, and all eyes were on us. I smiled because no matter who it was, it just wasn't the eyes I wanted to see.

"Bitch, who you looking for? Rashad?" she asked me.

"I didn't hear you. What you say?"

I heard her ass. I just didn't want to answer her. Being that the speakers were roaring with the latest songs, it was easy not to hear her.

"You heard me."

The waitress brought our drinks and sat a bottle of wine on our table. She pointed to a table behind us. I turned around, and it was that nigga Dre and his homeboy, Darnell. Dre licked his lips, and I waved. He was looking sexy, but I wasn't trying to take it there with him. When he told me he knew Rashad, I had stopped calling and texting him.

"You know they're going to bring their asses over here," I told Serenity. Our song "Motor Sport" by Migos, Nicki Minaj, and Cardi B came on. We got up and danced. The dance floor was too packed to be dancing.

I looked toward the door because there was too much commotion. Sure enough, it was Hakeem and Rashad. Bitches acted as if they were some damn celebrities walking in. I showed Serenity, and she chuckled. I knew she loved that nigga. I saw it in her eyes, but I was no better. I wanted Rashad in the worst way.

"Damn," we heard from behind us. I turned around, and it was Dre.

"Sup, sexy," he said, licking his lips.

"Sup."

"What's up, Serenity?" he asked her.

"Hi, Dre. How you been?" she asked.

"Good, just seeing what's good with your girl. I ain't heard from her in minute."

"I been around, just working and doing me," I told him.

"Come holla at me when you get a minute," he told me.

"I got you."

He walked away, and I smiled. It wasn't long before I noticed Rashad and Hakeem walking up to them, giving them some dap. Rashad looked at me and gave me a head nod. I smiled and turned away.

"Your baby daddy over there," I told her.

"I'm not blind, bitch."

I laughed and felt a pair of eyes on me. I looked to my right and saw two guys staring our way. I'd never seen the guy before, and he looked damn good. He fingered for me to come over, and I had to think about it. I peeped his boy, and he was looking just as fine.

"Aye, bitch. This nigga want me to come holla at him. Come with me."

She looked over at him and looked back at me.

"Bitch, those niggas fine as fuck. Let's go."

I knew she was feeling her drinks, but I also knew she wanted to make Keem jealous. We got up and walked over to where they were.

Serenity

I was feeling my drink, and seeing Keem stare at me, I wanted to show out. When Shay told me that somebody asked her to come holla at them, I looked to see who she was talking about, and I knew I had found the one. I needed somebody on the same level as Keem to make him jealous. Once we sat down, they introduced themselves.

"Sup with y'all. I'm Sacar, and this my homie, Moni. What's your name, beautiful?" Sacar asked me.

"Serenity... and this my best friend, Shayla."

"Shayla, huh? Come let me holla at you," Moni told her. She sat next to him, and they asked if we needed another drink. I damn sure didn't, or else I would end up fucking his ass on the table.

"Nah, we good. Thanks though."

I sat down, and Sacar was all up on me talking.

"So I've been here for about a month. How come I ain't never seen your sexy ass?"

"Well, this my first time here. I haven't been out in a while, but I needed some excitement, so me and my girl came out tonight."

"That's what's up, you got a man?"

"No, I'm single at the moment."

"Single huh? I was hoping you were because the way all these niggas up in here staring at you, I thought for sure one of them was your man, especially that nigga, Hakeem."

Hearing him call out my baby's daddy name had me wondering if he knew him well.

"How you know Hakeem?"

"I don't. I know of him. I heard he got these streets on lock."

I don't know if it was the way he said it, but it made me think he had something against Hakeem. That comment rubbed me the wrong way.

"So where you from?" I asked him.

"Baltimore," he said.

"Oh okay."

"I hate yelling over this damn music. What are you doing tomorrow?" he asked.

"Um, nothing really. I don't have any plans."

Let's meet up... maybe lunch or dinner and get to know one another."

"Okay, that's cool."

We exchanged numbers, and he kissed my cheek. I smiled but wondered why he was doing all of that.

"That nigga staring at us, so I wanna make sure he knows you're mine."

Oh, he knows I'm not. Trust me, I thought.

"When did I become yours?" I asked.

"Oh, I'll make it happen."

"You got a girl?" I asked him.

"Nah, I'm single, but I'm trying to change that. You gon' help me with that?"

He licked his lips, and I was instantly turned on. I had completely forgotten about Hakeem being on the other side of the club. Sacar's cologne was captivating, and I couldn't turn away from him if I wanted to. His dark smooth skin was begging me to lick it. His dreads were perfectly braided back. He had muscles, which I prayed one day I could wrap myself in. I knew he was tall, even though he was sitting.

"Maybe, but I would like to get to know you first."

"Oh, I plan to make that happen, sexy. You're so fucking thick. I bet that pussy taste good, don't it?" he asked in my ear. Being so close to him was unbearable. I hadn't had sex with anyone but Hakeem, but there was a need for change.

"I don't know. Maybe if things go well, you'll find out."

He licked my ear, and I smiled and giggled like a damn school girl. I looked over at Shay, and she was so caught up in whatever Moni was spitting in her ear. I laughed because it could be possible that they were spitting major game at us, but I was not trying to solve that in one night.

I noticed Rashad walking over to us, and I called Shay's name. Rashad was fine as well, but he and Hakeem were deadly. I wasn't blind to the fact that my baby daddy was a savage and a dope boy. People often referred to him as the plug, but I felt he was the damn socket, and he wouldn't hesitate to off a nigga if needed. Dex gave Keem his empire, and Keem ran that shit like he had built it from the ground himself.

"So I invite you out, and you over here chilling with another nigga? How that work?" Rashad asked Shay. I knew Shay wasn't gon' say anything slick to Rashad, especially in front of Moni, but if it was any other dude, she would have laughed at him.

"Rashad, you can't be serious right now."

"I'll give you two minutes, and then I'll show you how serious I am," he told her and walked off. I saw Keem looking over, and I knew he was just itching to put a nigga in their place. He lived for that shit.

"I'm not trying to start anything, so I'm just going to go 'head and get ready to get out of here. Moni, I enjoyed getting to know you and your company."

"Damn, baby. That's your nigga or something?"

"It's complicated is what it is. But like I said, I don't want any drama, so let's just connect another time."

Moni looked at Sacar and then smiled.

"Baby, I promise there'll be no drama if you stay. I know you don't know everything about me, but I'm that nigga. Ask around about me, and you'll find out exactly what I'm about."

"I think it's best we just leave," she told him.

"We?" Sacar asked.

"Yes," I intervened.

"You know what? Y'all right. I'm not trying to have any problems either tonight. Being that the niggas seem like they're ready to jump stupid, I'm gon' let y'all roll."

We told them bye and left. We had to walk past Hakeem and Rashad to get out because there was no exit by us. I felt Hakeem's eyes burning a hole in the side of my face. I tried walking as fast as I could.

Once we made it outside, someone started fighting. It looked like the chick Hakeem talked to. It wasn't long before him and Rashad came running out. I knew he wanted to make sure it wasn't us.

"Y'all good?" Keem asked.

"Yeah, it's not us. It's your bitch that's fighting," Shay told Keem. He walked toward the fight and sure enough, he saw that it was Rika and some other chick fighting.

Shay and I walked closer as well to get a better look and

listen in on what was going on.

"Bitch, stay away from my man. I don't give a fuck about you sucking his dick!" Rika yelled at him. I shook my head. He just couldn't get right. When I saw him pull Rika away from the chick, my heart fluttered. I felt some type of way, but I dismissed it.

I looked to my side and didn't see Shay. I turned around, and she was talking with Rashad. I smirked when she gave me that look. I already knew what it was. She walked toward me, and I started shaking my head.

"Bitch, you about to get the dick. I know."

"Serenity, don't be mad. You know I love that nigga, but here's my keys. Just go back to my crib. I'll be there shortly."

"Who you think you're talking to, Shay? You know damn well you aren't coming home no time soon. He's going to curse your ass out about being in another nigga's face, and then you're going to play that innocent role. Then, he's going to fuck the shit out of you," I told her.

"Well damn. What… you writing our love story? Can you write a part in there for yourself about getting some dick tonight?" she snapped back. We laughed, and she gave me her ticket to get the car from valet. I glanced over and saw Rika all in Keem's face, yelling at him. As the car pulled up, I got in and took off.

I stopped to get something to eat because I was hungry and thirsty. Once I made it to Shay's house, I thought about her alarm. She had activated the alarm for the house before we left, and I didn't know the code. I called her, and she didn't answer. *I'll eat my food, and if she doesn't call when I'm finished, I'll just go home for the night. Ain't like she coming back anyway,* I thought to myself.

After eating and still not hearing from Shay, I drove home. Hakeem's house was further out, so it took forty minutes to get to his crib. I played my songs and drove Shay's car as if it were mine. She had a nice Dodge Charger, and I wanted a car of my own as well.

Damn, this nigga here, I thought to myself as I pulled up. Hakeem was home, and I prayed he had fallen asleep. I didn't feel like dealing with his drama or him. I knew he would ask about the dude I was talking to at the club. Just thinking about Sacar made me smile.

I walked into the house and locked up. I figured I'd just go to my room and lock the door. I walked past Naomi's room and saw a few toys laying around. I shut her door and walked off. As soon as I got close to Keem's room door, Rika was walking out. We stood face to face.

"Hakeem, you really put it on me. I think it's because it was on your bed," she said. I knew she wanted to get under my skin, but I wasn't about to show her how pissed I really was.

"I think you just love the fact of being in my bed," he said from his room.

"No, Daddy. I love you."

She smiled.

"You know I got love for—"

His facial expression changed when he saw me. I looked at him and at his bitch and walked away.

"Serenity!" he called out to me.

"Why the fuck you calling her name? Let the bitch go to her room. Now that she finally got her little degree, she can get a job and move out."

I know this nigga ain't pillow talking about me to this bitch, I thought. I didn't even entertain them. I just shut the door behind me and locked it. I was jealous, hurt, confused, and scared. He had just asked if I ever thought about trying it again with him, and now he was back with her. *Maybe he never left to begin with, so that means I am the side chick.* I thought long and hard about my next move. I had to get my shit together and move out. I was giving myself a month, and that was it.

Hakeem

After pulling Rika off Vetta, I had to do damage control. Vetta had exposed everything we'd done a few days ago to Rika, and Rika beat her ass. She started yelling at me about keeping my dick in my pants and leaving me. I laughed because she wasn't going anywhere. After calming her down, I took her back to my place and hoped that would make her forget all the shit Vetta told her, even if it was only a few minutes. I fucked the shit out of her and had her cummin' all over my sheets.

After getting my shit on, I was about to head over to Rika's house with her, but when I came out the room, Serenity was standing face to face with Rika. I prayed Serenity didn't fuck her up, because Rika wouldn't be able to handle Serenity. Serenity could fuck with the big dogs when it came to fighting. Even though Rika could fight, Serenity would give her ass a go.

I made a few moves and headed back to Rika's house with her. I felt like shit for bringing her to the crib and Serenity catching my ass. I thought she was staying at Shay's crib. I knew she was hurt. I saw it in her eyes, but part of me was upset seeing her all in another nigga's face. I'd never seen that nigga before, so I wondered where she knew him. They seemed well acquainted.

It was early Saturday morning, and Rika hadn't gotten up. She didn't cook, so we always ate out. That's what I missed most about being with Serenity. She cooked every day for a nigga. I got up to shower and knew I had to handle business with Rashad and the crew, but I needed to speak with Serenity first.

Once out the shower, I noticed Rika sitting on her bed, looking at her phone. When she noticed me, she asked where I was going.

"I got to handle some street business, and check on Sere—"

Damn, I'm digging a bigger hole for myself, I thought.

"I have to check on Naomi and run a few errands. I'll get up with you later."

"You fucking her still, ain't you?" she asked.

"Who?"

"Hakeem, keep playing with me. You know what the fuck I'm talking about! You're still fucking Serenity, ain't you?"

"Nah, we ain't fucking."

She got out of her bed and went into her bathroom. I dropped a stack on her bed and left. I called my mom to check on Naomi, and she said Serenity had come to pick her up because she wanted to spend time with her today, and Naomi wanted to go.

"What? Why you didn't call to tell me that?" I asked.

"Because Serenity is her mother."

"I'll call you later, ma."

"Hakeem, is everything okay?" she questioned.

"Yeah, I'll hit you back."

I hung up and called Serenity's phone, but of course I was sent to her voicemail. I didn't know why I was nervous, like she would kidnap Naomi and leave the state of Texas. I just needed to give her some space and talk with her when she brought Naomi home.

I called Rashad and met him at the hub. It was hot as hell,

and I needed a blunt or a drink to calm my nerves.

"Nigga, you glowing and shit. What's up with your ass?" I asked Rashad.

"Before we get into all of that, I told your ass it's always some shit with you and Rika. I'm glad I did drive my own shit last night."

"Man, Vetta's ass just pissed that I stopped fucking with her ass, but tell me why you're glowing before I tell you what happened to my ass last night."

"Bitch, ain't nobody glowing, but I did fuck Shay last night. Man, that shit be so good. On some real shit, I am going to make shorty my girl. She's the one."

"Well, I'll be damned. I don't even want to tell you what happened and ruin your happy moment of love."

We laughed, and he pushed me back as we sat down on the step at the hub. Little beads of sweat started forming on my forehead.

"Last night, I took Rika back to the crib. To make a long story short, Serenity popped up and caught us walking out of the room."

"Damn, man. You right. You did ruin my moment."

"On life, man, I think she's going to move out on a nigga."

"Where she gon' move to? She just started working."

"I can feel it. Shit about to change, and I know she's going to want to keep Naomi."

"You know I love you like a brother, so I'm going to keep it all the way real with you. You fucked up, nigga. How you gon' tell her about not bringing people to the house when you go and do the shit? Not only that, but Serenity ain't even like that, so you didn't even have to tell her that. You won't even let her date, because you say you don't want a nigga knowing where you stay, but what I think is that you still love that girl and want her for yourself. You want your cake and to eat it too. I agree. She had a lot of time to get her shit together, but you the one told her she didn't have to work and that you would provide for her and Naomi, so that's all on you. Rika is a fucking snake. I can see that shit with a blindfold on."

I heard what he said, but I wasn't feeling how he was coming at me, even if everything he said was true.

"Whatever, man. I got a few errands to run. I'll holla at you later."

"I know your soft ass feelings hurt, but get your dick out of your ass, and man up. She ain't gon' keep dealing with your shit. Mark my words."

I jumped in my ride and sped off. I tried calling Serenity again, but she didn't answer. I knew I had fucked up. I just needed to fix it, and things would be back to normal. I just needed to talk with Serenity.

I called my big homie because I needed an escape from life, and every time I went to visit him, I always felt better. No matter what the subject was, he always spoke positive words to me.

"Well hello, Hakeem," Adrianne greeted as she opened the door. Dex and his wife stayed in a mansion about an hour from me. Adrianne was bad as fuck and always showed great hospitality when I came over.

"Sup, Adrianne. I just came to visit the old man."

I laughed. Dex was thirty-five, and Adrianne was twenty-eight. I just called him old sometimes because of his receding line.

"He's in the back. You know where to find him. How is that pretty girl of yours?" she asked.

"Oh, you know me and Serenity broke up years ago," I told her.

"I know, and I was talking about Naomi," she said, looking

at me sideways.

"Oh, yeah. Naomi is good... too smart and too grown for her own good."

"I just bet she is. You'll have to bring her next time. Dex claims he is her godfather, but we never see her."

"She is my goddaughter. It's his mother who is always keeping the child hostage," Dex stated, coming into the room.

"Sup, son?" he joked.

"Just came to holla at you. I haven't talked to you in a while."

"Well, come on back. It seems like you came to talk to my wife, as much time you just spent with her."

Dex and I joked around like that all the time. He always said he knew I liked his wife. She was fine but just not my type. She was mixed with Spanish and Black, and she had ass.

"Man, fuck you, but I'm going through some shit right now," I told him as he shut his office door.

"Street related or personal?"

"Personal."

"Okay, what's up?"

I sat there about an hour, talking about all the shit that was going on with me, and he sat there drawing on a damn paper, but I knew he was listening. After I finished, he held the paper up, and it was stick figures of three people.

"What the fuck is that?" I asked, about to laugh at his ass.

"This is you, Serenity, and Naomi. Everything you told me comes down to this. You want a family, and you just don't know how to establish that, but what you got going on now isn't going to work, nor are they healthy relationships. You have to find out how to make that all happen. Now this Rika chick, she's fine, but what else is she to you?"

I didn't answer, and I didn't even have one, to be honest.

"Don't wrack your brain, man, but keep doing what you think is best. When you finally find the answer, everything will work itself out, and you'll know what you need to do."

I shook my head and chatted about a few other things I wanted to discuss with him that were more business related.

Shayla

I was listening to SZA's "The Weekend" song while cleaning my house. I had spent the night and most of the morning with Rashad. He had my ass climbing the walls. It was funny because everything Serenity said was going to happen had happened. He cursed me out about being in another nigga's face, and I played innocent like it wasn't shit. Then, he started kissing me and taking my clothes off. I thought I heard Sacar tell Serenity he knew Hakeem and Rashad, but I guess he didn't, because Rashad didn't know who he was.

I was shocked when Rashad asked me to spend the day with him. I knew he just wanted to fuck me good throughout the day, so I declined his offer. A part of me felt like he did like me a little, but sometimes, I wasn't sure if he just liked the sex we had.

My doorbell rang, and I knew it was Serenity and Naomi. She had called and said she would be over to bring my car back and to talk with me.

I opened the door and didn't expect Rashad to be standing there. He was looking so sexy. Even though I woke up to him and saw him get dressed, I couldn't help but admire how fine he was. Rashad was a caramel color with hazel eyes. His curly short fro was black with dark blonde highlights at the end of them. At 27 he was about six feet tall to be exact and built. I loved his chest and six-pack. I swear he stayed in the gym working out, but he said he worked out at home, which he did have a gym inside his home. His red pinkish lips were asking me to kiss them.

"Hey, Rashad. What's up?"

"You got a minute to talk?"

"Yeah, come in."

I let him in and got a whiff of his cologne. He was smelling so good that I just had to kiss him one time before he said whatever bullshit he was about to say.

"Damn," he said, kissing me back.

"I just had to. You came over here looking all sexy and shit. I just had to kiss you."

"I'm trying to have you kissing on me all of the time," he stated. I didn't know what to say. He made comments like that all of the time, and we just ended up in bed together.

"So what's up?"

He pulled me to my couch, which was different. I hope he wasn't going to tell me he had an STD or something.

"I know how you feel about me, and I feel the same about you. I know you think I be out there fucking all types of bitches, but I don't. Yeah, I have a few but not how you be saying. I want us to be together on some exclusive shit."

"What you mean by exclusive?" I asked.

"Just me and you, baby girl."

I couldn't help but smile. All I wanted was for us to be together. He already knew everything there was to know about me, but he just couldn't leave those bitches alone.

"So you're saying you want me as your girlfriend and that you're going to be faithful?"

"That's exactly what I'm saying. Last night just did it for me. I can't let another nigga come scoop you up and make you his girl. You're mine and always going to be mine."

Damn, I love this nigga, I thought to myself. I started to cry, and he pulled me onto his lap. He wiped my tears and kissed my lips.

"Now, you can kiss me all you want."

He smirked.

"Oh, I plan to."

I was just about to kiss him when my doorbell rang.

"Who that?" he asked.

"Serenity and Naomi."

I opened the door, and Naomi jumped into my arms and kissed my cheek.

"I missed you."

She hugged me.

"Did you? Well, I missed you more, princess."

I sat her down and looked at Serenity. Her eyes looked puffy, and she looked sad.

"Hey, girl. What's up?"

"Nothing. I didn't know you had company," she said.

"I was just about to leave," Rashad said, walking over to Serenity.

"Uncle Ra-Ra, what you doing over here?" Naomi asked.

"I was just visiting Shay," he told her.

"Uncle Ra-Ra, you like my god mommy, Shay. That's what you told daddy last time."

We all burst out laughing because she was just too damn grown.

"I do like her. That's why she's my girlfriend now."

The face Naomi made was priceless.

"Oh my God. You can't have two girlfriends, Uncle Ra-Ra."

"Go sit your grown butt down, before I whoop your ass," Serenity intervened, and I just laughed it off.

"On that note, I'm out. I'll holla at you later, baby," Rashad told me. We kissed, and he left.

"What the fuck did I miss?" Serenity asked.

"Mommy, bad word," Naomi said.

"Go play in your room," she told her. I had a room for Naomi for when she came to visit. She was my goddaughter, and I loved her as if she was my own.

"That child of mine," Serenity said.

"So Rashad asked me to be his girl, bitch."

"I knew it was coming. Y'all just can't keep y'all hands off each other. I'm happy for you two."

"Thanks, but next subject. What's wrong with you?"

She sat down on the couch and looked in my eyes. I was starting to get concerned. I had never seen that look in her eyes.

"When you didn't answer last night, I had forgot to ask you about the code to your alarm so that I could disarm it when I got in. I just decided to go home... well... back to Hakeem's house. When I get there, Rika's bitch ass comes walking out of his room."

"Hold up. Wait. Stop!"

I had to pause the conversation because last I knew, they both had agreed not to bring anyone over. It was more for Hakeem because he didn't even want Serenity to date while living with him.

"So he had that bitch in the house?"

"Yes."

"So this nigga thinks that he can fuck you and turn around and bring her hoe ass to the house?"

"The bitch had the nerve to talk shit, talking about since I got my degree, I can get a job and move out."

"How the fuck she know you got a degree? Girl, I dislike Hakeem more and more."

"He had to been pillow talking with the bitch about me. I can just imagine what he be saying. I am so over this shit though. I can't go back there."

She started crying, and that was the last thing I wanted to see was my friend crying over her sorry ass baby daddy.

"Nope! Stop! Don't you dare drop one tear over that crooked foot nigga. Fuck him. Call that nigga Sacar, and get to know him. He's fine as hell, and the way he was all over you, I know he wants you."

"He wanted to meet up today for lunch, but I didn't get a chance to call him back."

"Well, go to dinner. I'll watch Naomi, and don't you even consider how Hakeem is gon' feel."

"Okay. Can I stay here for a few days?"

"Are you really asking me that?"

She shrugged, and I hugged her. She called Sacar, and they made plans for dinner. I went out and bought snacks for Naomi and I and planned to watch her favorite cartoon movie, *Moana*.

Serenity had been gone for about three hours, and Naomi was asleep. Rashad called, checking on me, and he stopped by. He asked where Serenity went, and I didn't tell him shit. Boyfriend or not, he was still Hakeem's homeboy. He left and wanted to spend Sunday together, and I told him I was free.

I heard a loud banging at my door. I thought about grabbing my gun, but I didn't live in a bad neighborhood, so I just looked out the window. I saw Hakeem's car and just shook my head. I opened the door, and he walked in, pissed.

"Yo, why the fuck I get a call from one of my peoples telling me that Serenity out with some nigga?"

"First of all, lower your fucking voice in my house. Second, are you sure they didn't say Rika? That's who your girl is, right?"

"Shay, stop fucking playing with me, and where she got Naomi at?"

"Naomi is sleep in her room."

"So she out here hoeing around and just dropping off my damn child to anybody?"

"Nigga, how you fucking sound? Serenity ain't no hoe, and she didn't drop Naomi off no damn where. I volunteered to watch my goddaughter."

"Hakeem, why are you here?" Serenity asked, walking in.

"Don't come in here asking questions. I'm here to get my damn daughter. You out eating dinner with niggas and shit. You ain't have the decency to call and let my daughter talk to me."

I was waiting for her to slap the shit out of his ass so that I could jump in and beat his ass.

"Your daughter was at her granny's, where she would still be if I hadn't gotten her. Your ass wasn't thinking about her last night when that bitch was all in the house!"

"So that's why you out there being a hoe, because Rika was at my crib, the crib where I pay bills at? You can't be mad my girl was at my house."

I saw the hit coming before he did. He couldn't even block it in time.

"Fuck you, Hakeem, and you're right about one thing. It is your house, and I won't be returning."

She walked off, and he tried going after her, but I stopped him.

"Nah, player. You already know. This my house where I pay the bills, so you can fucking get to stepping. "

This nigga looked me dead in the eyes and told me, "I don't care who pays the bills in this bitch. Wherever Naomi lays her fucking head, I'm gon' be."

He tried walking toward the room again, but again, I stopped him.

"Don't make me go that way, Hakeem. I hate you for doing my girl like that, but I half way like you for being Naomi's father. You better just leave before I not give a fuck and call the police."

"So you'll call the fucking 45 on me?"

That's what we called the police.

"Yes, you're out of line by calling her out her name. You need to think about the shit you're doing. Rika is your girl, not Serenity."

He looked at me like he was hurt, but I didn't care about his feelings. Serenity's feelings were probably destroyed.

Sacar

When Serenity didn't answer my text about going to lunch, I thought maybe she wasn't really feeling a nigga, but she called and asked if we could do dinner. I had plans, but I put all of that on hold for her. We met at a restaurant called Bodec. They had good Italian food. When I asked where she wanted to eat, she said she didn't care. She mentioned that she loved Italian food, so I had to introduce her to the Bodec spot. Even though I only been in Texas for a month, I knew of all the good spots. Having money like I had, you could explore everywhere.

After eating dinner, we hit up a lil' jazz spot downtown in San Antonio. We weren't really feeling the soft music, but we got the chance to talk. She told me a lot about her and that she had a lil' shorty. She showed me pictures, and I had to admit that the child was gorgeous. She looked just like Serenity. I asked when I was gon' be able to meet Naomi, and she said it would be a long time. I respected that. That showed that she loved and protected her child. I knew I had to make her my woman. In due time, she would be. I just needed to handle relocating my business to Texas. That nigga Hakeem and his boy Rashad, had those streets on lock, my plan was to approach him and ask if we could possibly work together. If he declined, I was gon' take it.

Once we left the jazz spot, some nigga spoke to Serenity. She spoke back but looked as if she didn't know who he was. I asked who it was, and she said she didn't know but didn't want to be rude. I never got the chance to ask about her baby daddy to find out if he was the crazy type or if he was cool. It didn't matter. I just wanted to know what I was up against. We ended our night, and I told her I wanted to spend more time getting to know her. She said she did as well, and we planned to hook up again soon. Once she left, I called Moni up to get our game plan together.

"I think that Shayla chick fucking with that nigga Rashad," he said as we rolled the blunt in his living room.

"Why? Because what happened last night?" I asked.

"Hell yeah. That nigga gave her two minutes to get rid of me, and she got the fuck on down. I tried calling her, but it keeps going to voicemail. I think she's ignoring my calls."

"Yeah, I noticed how she got down. I saw how Hakeem was staring at Serenity. He wants her. That's for damn sure, but that's already mine."

"Y'all kicking it?" he asked.

"Not like that just yet, but she's already mine. In due time, I'll be fucking the shit out of her, but you get that info on Hakeem's stash houses?"

"From what Pete told me, they don't have one, and if they did, their shit discrete to where nobody in their crew knows about it but them."

"Damn. I gotta find a way to get at that nigga. I wanted to run up his spot first, and then I'd come to him on the business tip, but shit, we need to make it happen fast."

"I say just start putting the work out there. Fuck that nigga."

"I want to give him the opportunity to be a part of the team first, but if he ain't with it, I'll take it. He'll have no choice but to work for me.'

"I see how you thinking. Either way, it's a win for us."

"You damn right. We still shooting to Baltimore next weekend?" he asked.

"Yeah, I gotta get that bitch situated, and then I'll tell her I'm done."

"Tookie gon' fuck your ass up," he said, laughing.

Tookie was my girl when I stayed in Baltimore. We'd been together for eight years. When I went away to do that four-year bid, it wasn't even a good month before I heard she was getting dick down. When I got out, she tried acting like she'd been down to ride when I knew the truth. I had only been out for about three weeks when I picked her up just to get my dick wet. We got pulled over, and I had some dope in the car. I damn sure couldn't take that charge. She took it for me and only got a little under a year. Even though shorty did that for me, I still couldn't fuck with her like that. I decided to get her a crib with some cash to get her set up and on her feet before I told her it's over. She could only respect that.

"Shit, she can't say shit."

"What day she get out?"

"Monday. That's why I wanted to get this together over the weekend for her. It's the least I can do."

"Your ass crazy. Good luck with that."

"Let me go tell my girl goodnight," I told him. I got up and headed into his kitchen.

"Who? Tookie?" he asked.

"Nigga, fuck you."

I waited for Serenity to answer, but she never did. I was gon' have to tell her about that shit. When daddy called, she needed to answer. I was about to walk back into the living room when she was calling back.

"Sup, sexy?"

"Hey. I was bathing when you called."

"Damn, so you naked right now?" I asked.

"I'm not even going to tease you like that," she said.

"You right. Anyway, I just wanted to tell you goodnight, sweetie. That's all."

"Aww, that's sweet. Thank you. I needed that."

"Oh yeah? What's up?"

"Nothing. I'm just stressing a little, but it ain't nothing."

"Well, you know I'm here for you. Whatever you need, I got you."

"You're too sweet, but I'll be okay."

"Aight, call me tomorrow. I'm about to chill with my nigga for a bit before I head home."

"It better be your boy."

"It is, ma. Don't even worry about that."

We ended our call, and I went back into the living room. Moni had his phone to his ear, caking to some hoe. I grabbed another blunt and lit it up.

Hakeem

S hit was all bad in my life. I was missing Naomi like crazy. It was hard not seeing her beautiful face every day. I took her to school today since Serenity was working. That was another problem because Naomi's school was further away because of her being at Shay's house. I needed to talk with Serenity because the shit was getting ridiculous.

I picked Naomi up from school and took her out to eat. She talked about school and the fun she had. Then, she mentioned playing with some little boy, and I checked her lil' ass.

"Who is Jayden?" I asked, biting into my chicken at Wing Stop.

"Oh, Jayden is my boyfriend."

I damn near choked hearing her say that.

"Your boyfriend? What the hell you know about a boyfriend, Naomi?"

"Naughty word, Dad."

"Naomi, what did I just ask you?"

"Jayden is a boy, and he's my friend. Duh."

"Duh, my ass."

"Ohhhh, naughty word again. I'm telling Mom."

"Fuck your mom."

She looked at me like I had said the worst thing ever about her mother. I felt bad because I shouldn't have said that to her.

"I'm joking, Naomi. Daddy is just having a hard time."

"Why? Is it because Mommy won't come home?" she asked.

"Am I talking to a four or forty-year-old?" I asked her.

"Umm... four," she replied back. I called the waiter over so that I could pay and leave. Naomi was just too much for me.

In the car, Naomi was talking non-stop. I asked her what had been going on with her god mom and mother.

"Nothing."

"Naomi?"

She said *nothing* too fast for me, like she'd been coached to say that.

"I'll buy you more pretty dresses if you tell me."

"Mommy will be mad."

"No, she won't, because I won't tell her you told me."

"Well, god mommy Shay said bad words about you."

I laughed because I knew that was going to happen anyway. Shay and I used to be real cool. Even when Serenity and I broke up, she still referred to me as bro, but she eventually started going against me.

"And Mommy is always on her phone, texting and smiling. Oh, and god mommy Shay said that Mommy needs to put it on somebody. I don't know what she was talking about."

"Do you be sitting right in their face when they're talking?"

I knew damn well Serenity didn't let Naomi sit in folks' faces while talking, so it would be something new.

"No, Mommy makes me go to my room at god mommy

Shay's house, but I still listen."

I didn't say anything else. I turned the music on and drove home.

Serenity had called ten times asking where Naomi was, but I never answered. She texted saying that she was on her way. I was sitting on the couch when Serenity walked in. She was looking mad as fuck but sexy at the same time. She looked around for Naomi, and I pointed to the room. She walked toward her room, and I heard movement. I walked in to see what the hell she was doing.

"You're not taking my daughter back over there. That's too much for her to be dealing with. She has to get up early and leave extra early to make it way over this way for school. Come out here so we can talk."

"Fuck you, Hakeem. You're not going to control what I do with my daughter."

I wanted to go there with her, but I knew we needed to talk.

"I don't want to wake her. Please just come out here."

She walked off first, and I followed. I didn't quite know where to begin, but I had to be careful.

"First, I just want to apologize for sleeping with you. It was my fault. I shouldn't have taken it there. The last thing I wanted to do was confuse Naomi on what was going on between us. Staying with Shay is cool, but it's too much on Naomi. I know we got our problems, but at the end of the day, we do the shit for her. I know the shit I said to you at Shay's house hurt, but I'm sorry for that too. I appreciate you as Naomi's mother. My bad for having Rika up in here. I thought you were staying at Shay's that night, but the rule still stands… no company over whatsoever."

"I can't stay here, Hakeem. It's just too much for me, and it's real funny how you asked me if I thought about trying it with you again, and then we ended up in bed together, but that's not the bad part. What's bad is that you brought the hoe back here. Then, she started yapping off at the mouth about my business that she shouldn't have even fucking known. What, you be laying up with the bitch and talking about me?"

"I admit that I told her a few things about you, but it's always something positive. I wouldn't dog you to another bitch. Despite what you may think I say to her, I defend you around her."

"You defend me?"

"Yes, I do. Look, I know we're not going to agree on where you're staying, but Naomi is staying here, point blank period."

I walked off because I couldn't take her looking at me like she hated me.

"No. Let's get one thing straight. You're not going to continue to tell me what my daughter does and doesn't do, and before you throw money in my face, ask yourself... when was the last time you read her a bedtime story or gave her a bath?"

I thought about it for a minute, and it had been a minute, but I didn't see her point.

"You can't even remember. The things you buy her are material. She needs your time. I'm the one that cares for the child. I'm the one that takes her to the doctor. I'm the one that goes over words with her every fucking night. Me! Her fucking mother! So if anyone has to say anything about where Naomi goes, its's me!"

She walked away and gathered Naomi's things. I just sat there, stuck on stupid because I couldn't disagree with anything she'd said. I wanted to tell her to just stay and let Naomi sleep. I wanted to tell her that I was sorry for everything and that I still loved her, but I couldn't. Instead, I let her and Naomi walk out. I decided to call Rashad, since I hadn't heard from him.

"Sup?" he answered.

"Meet me at the hub," I told him.

"I was just about to call you. I'll be there."

Once we both arrived, I walked in. A few of our crew members were there doing their thing; counting money, bagging up, you name it.

"Sup, bro?" Rashad asked me.

"Shit, just came from my girl's house."

"Your girl? Who yo' girl, nigga?" I asked.

"Shayla."

"Damn, so you were serious?"

"I was, and she told me what happened."

"I know, man, and before you go there, I just want to apologize for the way I acted the other day. You were only telling me what I needed to hear."

"Yeah, I figured you were on your period or something," he joked.

"Man, fuck you, but you said you were about to call me. What's up?"

"Pete came to holla at me. He said some niggas been asking about us."

"Oh, word?"

"Yeah, he didn't give no names. He just wanted to put it out there."

"That's interesting. Dex said he heard that too, and he wanted to see who it was coming from. We already put the word out there."

"Cool, so what's good? You talk to Serenity?"

"She came, took Naomi, and dipped. We did talk for a hot second, but I didn't say shit I wanted to say."

"Your mom said you weren't good at expressing yourself."

I laughed so hard at that fool. He was too much for me, but I was glad he didn't take the shit personal.

"I heard everything you said. I'm just trying to figure all of this out."

"First thing first, get rid of that bitch Rika."

"You so funny, but I haven't even heard from her ass all day."

Rika

"Oh my God! Right there! Yess... ohh."

I met Moni a few days ago, and he was actually cool. His paper was long just like Hakeem's, and he didn't have a baby mama. I was so tired of Hakeem's bullshit. I rode by his house, and Serenity was walking out. He was carrying bags and helping the little one in the car. I didn't get a good look at her, but seeing them look like one happy family, I got pissed and hit Moni up. He asked to see me, and I ended up bouncing on his dick. It wasn't better than Hakeem's, but it was good, and he made me cum. He wanted me to spend the night, but I needed to go and call Hakeem to see where his ass had been all day.

I headed home, and on my way there, I called Hakeem.

"Speaking of the devil," he said.

"I didn't see your number come across my screen," I told him. Whomever he was talking to, they must have been talking about me.

"Where you at?" he asked.

"On my way home. Where you at?"

"At the spot with Rashad."

"I guess. Are you coming over tonight?"

"Nah, I won't make it tonight, and I have to be up early to

take Naomi to school."

"Where the fuck is here mama at?" I asked. I swear, he needed to kick that bum bitch out.

"She's working now, so I take Naomi to school."

I didn't see that coming. She was working and probably thought she had a chance to get with him. I was about to nip that shit in the bud.

"Hakeem, I don't like y'all little living arrangement."

"Rika, not tonight, I'm not in the mood for this shit."

I had to calm my nerves before I went off on his ass. That was actually why I went out and got some dick. He was playing house with his damn baby mama.

"I know you're sleeping with her. This shit doesn't even make sense. You worry about her more than you worry about me. I haven't gotten a call from you all day, but I bet you talked with her."

"We have a child together. I have to talk with her."

"Didn't you say Naomi could talk good? You really don't have to talk with her mom for shit."

"You acting real simple right now, and I ain't feeling this shit. Holla at me tomorrow."

I looked at the phone, and the nigga had hung up on me. It was cool though. I was going to have the last laugh.

Two months later...

Serenity

I had been working and saving up for an apartment. I had completed my internship at the prison and applied to a position that was posted. I got the call, and they offered me the job. The first person I told was Shayla and then Sacar. Sacar and I had spent an enormous amount of time together. Whether it was for hours or five minutes, he was really a nice guy, and I enjoyed his company. I could really see myself being with him. It had been two months since I'd been staying with Shayla. Hakeem bitched like he always did, but I didn't budge. I was in the right place to start looking for an apartment. I had already gotten a credit card to establish some credit, and things were coming together.

I decided to go to the mall and get Naomi a few things. I was so proud of myself. I couldn't wait to tell Naomi that we were getting another place, and she would have a princess room.

I was walking out of JCPenney when I noticed Rika walking up. I prayed she didn't start shit with me, because I would just give her the ass whooping she deserved.

"Look who it is," she said. I didn't say a word to her. I just walked into Kid's Footlocker, and of course she followed me.

"Shopping with my man's money? You're so pathetic."

"Rika, I advise you to get away from me."

"Why? You can't take hearing the truth? You know... I'm

going to tell you what he said. Hakeem can't stand the fucking ground you walk on, and he hates that he even had a baby by you. Every day, he says he wished that I was Naomi's mom, and being that you suck as a mother—"

She could talk about me all day every day, but what she wasn't gon' do was talk about Naomi. I punched her in the face, and she stumbled. I started punching her like she was a damn punching bag. She couldn't even get a punch in, because I kept socking her in her face and mouth. I was trying my best to shut her mouth up for good. I was pulled back and pushed into a corner. It was a security guard. They called the police, and Rika said she wanted to press charges. I laughed because she was so damn stupid. Her dumb ass followed me into the store. I was trying to avoid her. The store manager was mad because blood was on some of the socks that were stocked. Rika told me to stay away from Hakeem, or she would kill me. I wasn't afraid, but the way she said it, I knew I had to be more cautious.

I sat in jail, pissed as fuck. I knew I had basically fucked my career as a social worker. When I got my phone call, I was about to call Hakeem when I hung up and called Sacar. He came and bailed me out. I cried in his arms, and he said everything would be okay. He had a friend that could get everything taken care of for me. I didn't see how when Rika pressed charges, but if they'd viewed the cameras, they'd see that she was picking with me first.

He took me back to the mall to get my car. I called Shay on the way there, and she was worried sick. I told her I was okay and that Sacar had bailed me out. As we pulled up to the mall, I thanked him and told him I would pay him back.

"Ma, don't insult me like that. I already told you that I got you. Go handle business with your family. I am sure they're worried about you. Hit me up later."

He opened my door and hugged me. I kissed him, and he squeezed my ass.

"Damn, I want your sexy ass."

I wanted him too, but we had to wait for all of that. I left and headed over to Shay's. While driving, Hakeem called, and I was hesitant to answer. Being that he had Naomi, I answered anyway.

"Hello."

"Yo, what the fuck is wrong with you? You trying to ruin your career before it even starts? Do you not think about the choices you make before you do them? Everything you do affects Naomi."

I couldn't believe he called me saying that shit. At first, I didn't want to believe what Rika was saying, but the way he talked to me, I believed every word. I hung up on him as I pulled up to Shay's house. Shay hugged me as soon as I got in.

"Did you beat that bitch's ass?" she asked.

"Beat the breaks off that hoe," I stated. We laughed, and I was glad I had Shayla. She always turned a bad situation into something funny. I bathed and asked if she could call Hakeem and let him know Naomi could just stay the night with him. She walked off and came back ten minutes later.

"Your baby daddy is crazy as fuck. He said he is on his way with Naomi, and he asked did I bail you out. I told him no. Your boo did."

"Shay, why you tell that man that? You know he's fucking crazy."

It wasn't long before someone started banging on her front door. I knew he couldn't have made it to her house in that amount of time. Shay walked away, and I closed the door quickly to get out the tub and dry off. Before I could do anything, the bathroom door swung open. Hakeem shut and locked it behind him. All I had was the towel that I quickly wrapped around me.

"Where is Naomi?" I asked. I was somewhat scared.

"With her god mommy, but now it's my turn to ask a question. Who the fuck bailed you out of jail?"

"Hakeem, it doesn't even matter."

He walked closer to me, and I backed up.

"Serenity, don't fucking play with me. Shay said it was your boo. Who the hell is your boo?"

"The only person you can question is your bitch. You wanna snap on me about beating her ass, but you the one telling her shit… talking about you hated having a baby by me and that you wished she was Naomi's mom. You know how bad that shit hurt?"

"That bitch said what!" he yelled out. I tried walking around him, but he blocked me. I moved back, remembering I only had a towel on.

"I would never say no shit like that. That bitch lied to you. Why the fuck would I tell her some shit like that? She told me you started fucking with her at the mall."

I just stared at him. He knew me better than that. I would never go looking for drama.

"I'm so sorry, Serenity. This shit getting out of hand. I'm gon' handle Rika, but I hope you know I would never talk down on you to anybody. I never have and never will."

I just couldn't take it. I started crying because it was just too much. I just wanted him out of my life. He walked closer to me, and I backed into the sink. I had nowhere else to go.

"Tell me you believe me, Serenity… that I would never talk down on you to another bitch."

I didn't speak, and he got closer.

"Tell me," he demanded. He tugged at the towel, and I tried pushing him back. He didn't move an inch.

"Hakeem, move."

"No, not until you tell me you believe me."

"It doesn't even matter anymore."

"It does because you should know me better than that."

"I should know you better than that? Hakeem, I don't know who you are anymore."

"You do."

He got closer, and I was damn near in the sink. He kissed my neck, and I tried pushing him with more force. He yanked the towel away, and I covered myself with my hands.

"Stop, Hakeem. This isn't right."

"It is right."

He lifted me onto the sink and got between my legs. I was so nervous that I couldn't even think straight.

"No. Stop, Hakeem."

"Tell me you believe me."

He kissed my neck, and all I could do was close my eyes.

"Stop," I cried out.

"Why?"

I didn't give him an answer. Tears just started coming down my eyes. His lips latched on to mine, and he kissed me. My lips had a mind of their own because I started kissing him back. He removed his dick from his pants and eased inside of me. My walls clenched on as if they were welcoming him.

"You're the only one trying to reject me. Your pussy welcomed me with open arms," he said. I closed my eyes and bit my lip as he pumped in and out of me.

"Tell me," he said.

"I… I believe you."

I finally let go. I dropped the soap dispenser on the floor, trying to reach for something to grab on.

"Fuck!" I yelled out.

"Y'all good?" Shay asked on the other side of the door.

"Yeah, we straight. Damn, this pussy wet as fuck," Hakeem revealed.

"What the fuck? Is y'all fucking?" She asked.

I couldn't speak, because I had to mask my moans. The shit felt so good, and I came all over his dick. After staying in the same position for a few minutes, he let me down, and I couldn't believe what had just happened. He washed up, got himself together, and walked toward the door.

"I'll let Naomi stay here. I'll be back to get her for school tomorrow."

He opened the door, and Shay was standing at the door. She looked at him, and he smiled. I quickly grabbed the towel to cover myself.

"Hakeem, ain't shit funny. You in here fucking my friend, and you got a whole bitch on the other side of town. This shit ain't cool."

"Shut your ass up. I'm done with that bitch. I'm going to go handle her ass now."

He walked away, and I quickly got myself together. I heard him tell Naomi goodnight. Once he left, I straightened up the bathroom and came out. Shay was on the couch, looking at her phone.

"Now that Naomi is sleep, what the fuck happened?" she asked.

"I told him what Rika said about him wishing I wasn't Naomi's mom, and he just snapped. He begged me to believe that he would never talk down on me. I told him I didn't know what to believe basically. I was in the tub when he got here, so I was drying off. I only had the towel on. That nigga snatched it away and started kissing on my neck and pulled his dick out. I couldn't have stopped him if I wanted to."

"Well, I'll be damned. I don't know what the fuck to say right now. What y'all fucked on, the floor?" she asked.

"On the sink," I told her, covering my face.

"I hope you cleaned my sink off, lil' nasty asses. What the fuck is y'all gon' do? Am I hating him or loving him? A bitch is confused on her role."

"I don't know. I don't know is all I can say."

"Do you still love him?" she asked.

"I never stopped."

"Y'all need to sit down and talk. Matter of fact, go now. It's not that late, and Naomi is sleep because when I wake up tomorrow, I need to know if I am hating Hakeem or loving him as a brother again. I'm not going to bed confused on my feelings because y'all wanna hump one day and kill each the next. Nope! We figuring this shit out tonight."

I couldn't help but laugh at her crazy ass, but she was right. I headed to his house. He said he was going to go and handle Rika, so I texted him and told him to meet me at his place. As I drove to Hakeem's, Sacar called me.

Hakeem

"**W**hy the fuck you tell her some shit like that? You know damn well I ain't never say anything bad about Serenity, let alone say I wished she wasn't Naomi's mother. You deserved that black eye and broken nose. You lucky it is already broken because I would beat your face in."

"Fuck you, Hakeem. You taking that bitch's side over me."

"You know what? I am taking her side. It's over between us. When you come for mine, shit gets real."

I walked out of her house, and she came to the door, yelling that it wasn't over and that she was going to fuck Serenity up when she saw her. I knew she wouldn't step foot to Serenity again after that ass whooping. I looked at my phone, and Serenity sent a text about meeting at my place.

I walked into my house, and Serenity was sitting on the couch. I knew she was still hurt and fucking her only made shit worse. I sat down and waited for her to speak.

"What are we doing?" she asked.

"I'm sorry, Serenity. I know I keep fucking up. On the real, I never stopped loving you. You pushed me away, and you wanted shit to end between us. Everything was good up until you wanted to break up."

"Shit wasn't good. You treated me more like your child than your woman. I had to do what you said when you said it. If you didn't like something, it was your way or no way at all. I'm not your child, and I won't let you run all over me. When I got the offer today for the job, you were the first person I wanted to call, but I couldn't, because you were on that bullshit."

"You could have still called. I had to hear it from Rashad."

"I just can't do this with you. I know it's a lot for Naomi with the back and forth. That's why I'm getting an apartment. I'm looking closer to her school."

Apartment? When did she decide all of this? I asked myself.

"So what? We're not going to try and work it out?" I asked.

"Why should we... because we fucked?"

"No, because I love you, and you love me."

"You have to change. Until I see that change, I can't even think about being with you."

"Who the fuck is this nigga you seeing?" I asked. It had just crossed my mind.

"That's not even relevant right now."

"Did you go see that nigga in my car?"

"That's exactly what I'm talking about. Stop throwing shit in my face. I know the car isn't mine."

"You right. My fault. But on the real you got me fucked up if you think I'll let you go see another nigga in the car that's mostly mine. Yeah, you drive it, but don't you see how fucked up that is?"

"It's nothing. We had a few dates, and that's it."

"A few dates?"

"Hakeem, please. I have the right to live my life."

I thought about it and thought about what Rashad and Dex said. Even though I was done with Rika, I had to let Serenity go as well.

"Aight, we'll figure the co-parenting thing out, I guess. I don't want lawyers involved, because I don't need the white people in my business."

"I agree."

"I don't want my daughter around no niggas, period."

"You don't have to tell me that, Hakeem."

I knew saying that pissed her off, but I needed to let her ass know. She got up and walked toward the door. Even though it was hard to let her go, I had to. If she wanted to see what else was out there, I had to let her. Maybe I wasn't the one for her. I just needed to make sure Naomi was good at the end of the day.

Once Serenity left, I called my mom. I told her everything that happened, leaving a few details out. She wanted to talk with Serenity and me together. I told her I would set it up and let her know when.

∞∞∞

I was driving Naomi to school to drop her off. She was too quiet, which was odd for her grown butt.

"Why are you so quiet back there?" I asked. She looked up, and I looked at her through the mirror. She didn't answer, and I started to worry that she was sick or something.

"Naomi, princess, what's wrong?"

"Mommy said that we're getting a new place to stay. That means that you two are getting a divorce."

Divorce? What Serenity teaching this girl, I thought to myself.

"Princess, we're not getting a divorce, because we weren't married, and it's best for Mommy to get her own place to live. That doesn't change the fact that we both love you more than anything, okay?"

"Okay, Daddy. Will you spend the nights with me there?"

I didn't want to tell her no, but I didn't want to say yeah and Serenity not be cool with it. I just nodded and pulled into her school parking lot. I got out and walked her inside. Once inside, she went to hang up her backpack. Her teacher walked over to me and smiled.

"Hello, Hakeem," she said.

"Sup, Ms. Steele?"

"I haven't seen Serenity in a while. Is everything okay?"

I knew the white bitch was just being nosy. I smiled, trying my hardest not to curse her ass out.

"Serenity started her new job, so I will be bringing Naomi to school in the mornings, and if I can't, Naomi's grandparents will. They're listed as authorized pick up and drop offs."

"That's great. Well, I hope you enjoy the rest of your day. Naomi is doing great. She is actually taking a few tests today. We think she is a too advanced for preschool. The words and phrases she uses are far more advanced than what is taught. I know Serenity works with her, and that is wonderful. However, we believe that kindergarten may be too relaxed as well for her."

"So what are you saying? You want to skip her to first grade?"

"It may be possible, but the test will determine that. I just wanted to give you a heads up. We will sit down with you and Mom of course and go over the results once they are formed."

"Okay. I must say that's good news and kind of scary, She's only four."

"I know, but let's talk when I have more information."

I peeked my head into the classroom, and Naomi was sitting down eating the breakfast they gave out. I smiled because my baby girl was a blessing to me, and I would protect her at all costs.

I sat inside of the hub with Rashad, asking him about him and Shay. He was really in love, and I was happy for him. Shay and I were good friends before Serenity and I got together. She didn't even know I was messing with Serenity until Rashad told her. She was happy with it until things changed between Serenity and me. After that, it was team Serenity, and fuck Hakeem. I wasn't tripping though. She was still sis, with her crazy ass.

"That's my baby, man. I love the fuck out that girl," he told me.

"I been knew that, nigga."

"So what's good with you and Rika?"

"Man, I broke it off with her, but I'm starting to miss that head she be giving me."

"Nigga, I know you ain't pressed for no head when bitches stay trying to serve you."

"You know how I feel about bitches. If I ain't choosing them, I don't fuck with them."

"So you really letting Serenity go?"

"Man, next subject," I told him.

"Here you go with that sensitive shit again. You can't even talk about it. It hurts that bad?"

"Get the fuck out of here. I'm just not trying to talk about it."

"This me, nigga. Just tell me this. You still want her, don't you?"

"If I wanted her, trust me... I would have her."

"I think you lost it. Serenity ain't fucking with you like that."

"What if I did say I do want her?" I asked him.

"I would say go get your girl."

"It ain't the right time right now. Her head in a different place. She thinks I changed and had the nerve to say I be trying to control her. All I did was help her out when she ain't have shit. She was fine as fuck, so I fell for her. We fucked, and she got pregnant. She wanted to get rid of it, so I told her I would take care of her. Now you know how I feel about a chick being in the club every damn weekend, so there were times when I told her she couldn't go, or if we had disagreements, I felt that by me being the man, what I said goes."

"That sounds controlling to me, bro, but what do I know?"

"I don't know what the future holds, but Naomi is my main focus right now."

"That's good. One thing I can say about you is that you're a damn good father. You may be a shitty ass boyfriend but a good father."

I laughed and got up to leave. It was a nice day, and the sun was beaming. I was looking good as fuck. I had to meet with Dex about some shit he wanted me to look into.

Driving to Dex's house, my phone started ringing. It was Rika. I answered without speaking.

"Hakeem, I know you're there," she said.

"What can I help you with?"

"Can we talk?"

"About?"

"I want to apologize and see you. I really miss you."

The tone in her voice did something to me. I had to admit that I missed her too. I told her I had to handle a few things and would call her if I decided to come by.

Rika

I was laid up with Moni all morning. Since Hakeem broke it off with me, I hit Moni up and kicked it with him. As soon as I made it to his crib, he started sucking on my pussy, and it was the best I'd had in a long time. Hakeem always acted like he didn't give head, which was dumb, but I didn't trip. At least I knew he wasn't giving that bitch Serenity any head. I let that bitch get the best of me, but I was prepared for round two. She had me fucked up if she thought I was going to let her walk away being the champ.

"Damn, I can fuck you all day," Moni, told me.

"I have to go, baby. I'm already late for work."

"I'll take care of you, sexy. Quit that job."

"I wish, but I'll come by tomorrow, and we can have sex all you want."

"Aight, bet."

We kissed, and I got my things and left. I really didn't have to work, but I wanted to call Hakeem and see if he would take me back. I know it seemed foul that I was fucking with someone else and trying to get him back, but I loved Hakeem, and he was the only man for me. I called Hakeem and he didn't say anything, but he answered the phone. I knew I had another chance, knowing he answered for me. I told him what I wanted, and he said he would hit me up if he decided to come. I knew he was coming, and I would be waiting with my legs wide open.

I had bathed and cleaned my house while I waited for Hakeem. It was a little after 5:30 p.m. When I thought that maybe he wasn't going to show, I heard a knock at my door. I removed my robe and ran over to the door. I had just gotten my hair done. I rocked a curly sew-in. He loved the look on me, so I knew he would approve. I wore some boy shorts and a crop top. I opened the door, and he stood there looking fuckable.

"Hey, Hakeem. Thanks for coming."

He walked in, and I shut the door behind him. He smelled so damn good, but I knew I smelled even better.

"I fucked up, and I shouldn't have told Serenity that shit. I was just jealous of her always being around you. She wakes up to you and goes to bed with you, even if it is not in the same bed. You're still there with her, giving her security while I'm sleeping alone at night, missing your touch. I just wanted to say that I'm sorry, and if you want me to apologize to her, I will."

I needed an Oscar for the performance I put on. I knew I had him when he smirked.

"Rika, that shit was foul as fuck. I never thought you would stoop that low to hurt anyone. If you would have just told me the way you felt, I would have handled it."

I been telling your ass how I felt about the bitch from day one, I thought to myself.

"Do you forgive me?" I walked closer to him, and he stared at me. I put my hands around his neck, and he pulled me in for kiss. I sucked on his tongue, moaning. He knew what I wanted.

"Aight, ma. You apologized like you said on the phone. I'm going to get going. I forgive you though."

"Can we start over? I can't live without you, Hakeem. I love you, and I need you, especially right now."

I stripped from my boy shorts, and he licked his lips. I

knew I had him. It was over for Serenity, and she could never have my man. He pulled out a condom, and I rolled my eyes, but I didn't want him to leave, so I let him use it on me.

"Right there, Hakeem. Don't move. Ahhhhh... Oh my God."

He hit my spot like a sniper. All my juices flowed onto him, and I couldn't stop there. I needed him in me all night.

"Spend the night with me, Hakeem," I requested.

"I can't, baby."

"Why not, Hakeem? This is why our relationship keeps failing. When I need you, you're not there."

"You're right, Rika, but I'll have Naomi tonight, so I can't."

"What you mean *have Naomi*? Where is her mother?"

"She has to work early tomorrow, so I'll have Naomi all night. Serenity moved out a few months ago."

Well I'll be damned. This is my chance to meet the brat and spend the night, I thought to myself.

"Can I spend the night? I want to meet Naomi anyway."

"I don't know about that. Naomi don't do well with new faces."

"Please, Hakeem. Give me that. If I can't meet her, I'll come when she's sleep. I promise to take good care of you."

"Aight, you can come when she's in bed. I'll hit you up when it's time. Don't be on no crazy shit. I'm not trying to be at odds with my baby mama over no dumb shit. She don't play that shit when it comes to Naomi. I think you found that out already."

Fuck that bitch. She's going to get hers soon.

"I'll be on my best behavior, and I can't wait to fuck in your bed. I love when your toes curl up."

"Stop it. I have to go though. I'll hit you up."

He left, and I did the money dance. It was as if I'd just hit the lottery. I packed my overnight bag and a few other things to leave there to mark my territory, just in case that bitch went snooping around.

Serenity

Naomi was staying with her dad because I had to go to work earlier than usual. I never knew how important social workers were in a prison environment. A lot of the prisoners deserved to be there, but there were a few that I felt were innocent and had just got caught up or were in the wrong place at the wrong time.

I sat in the living room with Rashad and Shay. They were so funny together. It didn't make any sense.

"Serenity, how you been?" Rashad asked.

"I've been good. Things are good. I'm training, so I'm still going through the motions at work, but everything is good."

"I hear you're seeing someone."

I shook my head. No matter how cool Rashad was, he was still Hakeem's homeboy.

"I don't know who your source is, but they're fraud."

I laughed, and he smirked.

"So why not be with Hakeem? You know that nigga loves you, right?"

"I'm trying to move forward, not backwards."

"So you think being with my boy is moving backwards?" he asked.

"Rashad, I'm not answering that. I know you two like the back of my hands. Y'all tell each other everything."

"I won't say shit. All I'm saying is if you love someone, you shouldn't think about it as going backwards. Just because y'all got history don't mean you can't move forward with them. Sometimes, when it comes back around, it's better than before anyway."

"Nigga, what? You been reading or something?" Shay asked. I laughed because I was thinking the same thing. Rashad had changed. It was a good change though.

"You're so different now, Rashad. What has gotten into you?" I asked.

"To be honest, I was tired of coming home to nothing. I got all this money, a nice house, cars, clothes, jewelry, and all of the above, but I was missing something, and that's Shayla. I always said when I settled down that she was gon' be mine. However, seeing her all in the club all up on another nigga did it for me. I had to get my girl. Fuck that player shit."

Shayla looked at me, and I looked at her. She blushed, and I knew it was true love.

"Aww, that's so sweet."

We all chatted, and I retired to bed. I had a few apartments I had scheduled to view, and I couldn't wait to find one and move in. I loved Shay, and staying with her brought us closer, but I needed my space, and I wanted to get Naomi adjusted. My phone was on the charger in the room. I texted Hakeem so that he could kiss Naomi for me. I tried closing my eyes to sleep, but my phone started ringing.

"Hello?"

"Sup, sexy?" Sacar asked.

"Hey, nothing… laying down. I have to be at work at 4:00 a.m. tomorrow. My training schedule is all over the place."

"Damn, that is early. Well, I won't keep you. I just wanted to hear your voice. I hadn't heard from you today."

"I'm sorry. I've been busy. I do want to see you though."

"This weekend, we should get away and have some alone time."

You mean fuck, I thought to myself.

"I don't know if I'll have a sitter for Naomi. Can I let you know later in the week?" I asked.

"You sure can. Get your beauty rest. Hit me up tomorrow."

"I will. Good night."

"Good night, sexy."

"Oh, wait," I told him.

"Sup?"

"Thank you."

"For what, baby. I told you not to thank me for treating you like a queen."

"For handling that shit for me. Your lawyer called the other day and said I was all good. They viewed the tape at the mall, and sure enough, they saw her following me."

"I told you it's nothing, and I also told you that whoever your baby daddy is, should learn to keep his hoes in check. They shouldn't feel it's okay to come fuck with his baby mama, whether y'all together or not."

"You're something special," I told him.

"Sweet dreams, baby."

I smiled as I hit the end button. He was just too good to be true. That's how Hakeem had started off in the beginning.

∞ ∞ ∞

I hit the snooze button one too many times. I quickly showered and got dressed. I grabbed my work bag, keys, purse, and phone and headed out. I was happy I had filled the tank up so that I could head straight to work.

"So what made you want to be a social worker?" Fallon asked. Fallon was the social worker coordinator who was training me. She was very nice and cool. I could see myself hanging with her outside of work. She was pretty, more of a bad bitch if you asked me. She was light skinned with a nice frame and just the right amount of ass and hips. Her chest was average, but she was beautiful and smart. Her hair was long, but she wore it up in a high bun. Her Chinese eyes and full lips really gave her an exotic look.

"I just love being able to feel there is a purpose for what I am doing. It's a privilege to be able to connect with people and find creative solutions to help them… the diversity, the love, the empowerment, and being able to see and feel the changes being made."

"I think you should have been a psychiatrist or something," she said. I laughed and told her that wasn't for me.

"Okay. Before we go in here, I have to tell you that this man is crazy as hell. He's going to make some nasty remarks, but all you need to do is continue asking the questions that are written. If he starts to say inappropriate things, just redirect him, and ask another question until he answers all four."

I looked at her like this was going to be a very long day. I was nervous but ready to show that I was capable of doing my job. We waited for the doors to open. Once we got in, there was a big table, and the prisoner sat on the other side. Seeing that he had cuffs on his hands and that his feet were chained. I felt much better. Fallon sat on the other side while I sat directly in front of him.

"Mr. Curt, we're here to ask you a few questions. As you know, you've been through this process before. My name is Serenity, and I am a social worker here at this prison. I will probably be working with you throughout your transition to home."

"You're new, huh? Yeah, we love new meat around here."

I swear he sounded as if he started smoking as soon as he left his mama's vagina.

"Excuse me, Mr. Curt. What did you eat today?"

"I didn't eat shit. Those fuckers took my meal because I didn't come in on time for count, but I would eat you in a heartbeat."

"That's inappropriate. Please, let's stay on track. If you could magically change something about your life, what would it be?"

"I would change the fact that I have a fucking big dick. Maybe I wouldn't be so damn horny all the goddamn time. It don't make it no better by them sending pretty bitches in here to talk to me, knowing damn well I can't touch them."

I wanted to laugh so badly, but I kept it professional and asked another question.

"You're in the process of going home in two months. What are your plans?"

"My plans? Let's see. I don't have no family, so I'll probably find me a lil' gig, get some money, and find me a woman. Other than that, I don't have any plans. I been in this hell hole for eight long years."

"Do you hurt anywhere?" I asked.

"No, not today. My legs were hurting the other day, but it stopped. My dick been hurting though. Can you look at it for me?"

"That's inappropriate. If you could magically change something about your life, what would it be?" I asked again.

"I would change the prison so that females and males can

be together."

"Mr. Curt, thanks for your time, and I will see you next month."

I got up and met Fallon by the door. I heard the guard call Mr. Curt, and they escorted him back to his cell.

"Girl, it's too damn early for this mess. I wasn't expecting that."

"I told you. I usually don't warn people when they go in, but I know you're new to this whole process. I must say, you did well. I was impressed," Fallon stated.

"Thank you. I can deal with that. It's threats of killing me that bothers me."

"I can deal with threats. It's people like Mr. Curt I can't deal with."

We laughed and headed to another room. We went over notes, and I did some progress reports on Mr. Curt. I looked at the time and wondered if Hakeem had woken up to get Naomi ready. I decided to send him a quick email from the tablet I held.

"What are you doing for lunch?" she asked.

"I don't know. I didn't have plans. You?" I asked.

"I started my diet months ago, and I'm doing well, but I want a burger today. I think I deserve one."

"That sounds good, but I'm thinking of something light today, either salad or soup."

"Well, you take your butt to Panera's Bread while I go get a burger."

I laughed and asked her how old she was.

"I'm twenty-four. You?"

"Guess?" I told her.

"Let say you're twenty-two or twenty-three."

"Nope."

"Higher?" she asked.

"Nope."

"You're not only twenty-one?"

"I'm twenty."

"What? really?"

"Yes, I started with basic college courses and eventually dropped out, but I finished online, and it was all year around online, so that's how I finished so fast."

"Wow, that's great. I'm proud of you. We should hang sometimes, outside of work."

"That would be great. What's your name on Facebook?" I asked. She gave me her name, and I wrote it inside of my notebook. We didn't have access to use our cell phones while in the prison. The tablet was the only thing we had.

It wasn't anywhere near close to lunch, but I needed to make sure Hakeem was up to take Naomi to school. Fallon and I walked off to our cars. She was parked a little further away from me. Hakeem didn't answer, so I called Shay to see if she was up getting ready for work.

"Hello?"

"Shay, you up?"

"Girl, yes. Rashad just not to long left, so I stayed up. What's up?"

"Can you stop by Hakeem's and see if he is up. I called him, and Naomi is taking a test to see where they're going to place her next year. Remember, I told you they told Hakeem she's too advanced for preschool?"

"I remember, and Serenity, that is out the way for me. That mean, I'll have to get dressed now and leave within twenty minutes."

"I know, but your goddaughter needs to be at school today. You know Hakeem sometimes sleeps through his alarm clock."

"You lucky I love Naomi. Oh my God. I hate you right now."

"I love you more. Thanks. Send me an email when you get in touch with him. My phone will be off."

"Yeah, yeah, whatever. Bye."

She hung up, and I laughed. I knew I owed her big time.

Shayla

I called Hakeem, but he didn't answer. I quickly did what I needed to do and left the house. I stopped at the gas station because I needed coffee. After that, I made my way to his crib. As I drove, I thought about the night Rashad and I had. We usually joked around and played with each other, but last night was a serious moment. He told me how much he really loved me, and he made love to me. At first, I thought he would still be the same nigga, but he proved he had changed. I deleted all the niggas I had in my phone, and he did the same with deleting females. It felt good knowing I was the only one.

I pulled onto Hakeem's road. I didn't know why his ass moved all the way in the Boonies. I was pulling in when I saw a woman and looked closely enough to figure out that it was Rika. I parked and stopped on the other side.

I didn't know if I should get out and confront him or call Serenity, but I remembered her phone wouldn't be on. I started talking aloud to myself.

"Bitch, just get out, and beat that bitch's ass. Naomi already knows I am crazy, so she'll be okay. No, Shay. Stay in the car, and just wait to see what is going to happen. Fuck this. Just get your phone out."

I pulled my phone out and started to video record. I knew he would eventually see me when he pulled out. Rika put Naomi's backpack on as if they were in a hurry. I looked at the time and knew Naomi would be late for school. Hakeem came out, only to run back in. I thought I had enough to show Serenity, so I smashed off before he came back out.

I didn't know if I wanted to send her the video while she worked. It would just have to wait until she got off. It was a sure to be a long day, and I wasn't ready to tell her the news, but he had life fucked up. I emailed her and told her Naomi was on her way to school.

After work, I had a few missed calls from Hakeem. I called Serenity first, and she had already made it back to my house. Something came over me, and I knew exactly what it was. It was my goddaughter. As much as I wanted to let Serenity see the video, I knew I had to just talk to Hakeem first and give him the chance to tell Serenity. If he didn't, I had the video to prove it.

"Sup, Shay?" he said into the phone.

"You busy?" I asked.

"Nah, about to grab Naomi in a bit and bring her over there. You called me early as hell. What's good?"

"I was calling because Serenity wanted to make sure you were up. She doesn't get service at work. You didn't answer, so I just came by."

"I was probably already gone when you came."

"Actually, I saw that bitch put a backpack on Naomi as if she's been around my goddaughter before. I sat there and watched you run out, only to run back in. Now, I could have told Serenity, but I wanted to give you the chance to tell her yourself. If you don't, I sure will, and before you say anything stupid, I have a video of everything. The ball is in your court, but I advise you to play smart."

"I'll tell her."

The call ended, and I shook my head. He knew not to play with me. I prayed shit didn't get too crazy, but I knew it wasn't likely.

At home, Serenity talked about work and her crazy day. She was dead tired from the early hours she had pulled. She told me about the Fallon chick, and I wasn't feeling any newcomers.

"Nah, I can't fuck with too many bitches. Your ass enough."

"Shut up, but she's cool. We all have to hang out. I promise you will like her."

"If that'll make you feel better, go right ahead."

"Where is Rashad?" she asked.

"Taking care of street business last time I checked."

It wasn't long before Hakeem and Naomi came walking in the door. He looked at me and didn't speak. I didn't care. He always got in his feelings when shit was on him. Naomi ran over to me and kissed my cheek. I hugged her and picked her up. She said she had already eaten and just wanted to take a bath and watch cartoons.

"Long day at school?" I asked.

"Yes, Jayden was sick, and I had to deal with the other kids all day by myself."

"Jayden? Who is Jayden?" I asked her. Before she could answer, Hakeem asked Serenity to ride somewhere with him.

"Aye, Serenity. Come take a ride with me. I need to holla at you about something."

"Ride with you? Hakeem, I am tired, and I don't feel like leaving to go anywhere."

"It's kind of important."

"Will you watch Naomi until we get back?" she asked.

"Stop asking crazy questions like that. You know I will."

They left, and I said a prayer. I went back to question

Naomi about the Jayden boy.

"He's a boy in my class. He's the only one that I like to talk to. All the other kids don't talk like us."

Yeah, she's a little too advanced, I thought to myself.

Hakeem

I couldn't believe the shit was happening. I had fucked up on a completely new level. Shit was about to get real, and I knew it. When Shay called and told me that shit, I knew it would go better coming from me. At least I could tell the whole story. Shay only could tell what she saw.

"So what's up, Hakeem? Why did we have to leave the house to talk?" she asked. Serenity was looking so beautiful her hair was up in a ponytail, and she had on some shorts and a simple T-shirt, but she still looked beautiful to me. I knew what I was about to say was going to piss her off. I didn't say anything until I reached our destination. It was a lake area. It was quiet, which was most cases on a weekday.

"Let's walk," I told her. We got out and walked down the sidewalk, viewing the lake. The sun had already set, and evening was coming to an end.

"Serenity, what I'm about to say is going to piss you off, but let me explain the whole story before you go off."

I saw the look in her eyes, and I had to tell her it wasn't what she thought.

"No one hurt Naomi."

"Okay, what is it?"

"Rika spent the night at the crib last night. She came over after Naomi was asleep. My phone somehow was turned off, and my alarm didn't go off. Therefore, I had to rush to get Naomi to school, so she kind of… in a way… met Rika. Rika rode with me to drop her off as well. I know it was stupid, and you don't have to worry about it happening again."

"You damn right because from now on, Naomi cannot stay at your house. If you want to see her, you'll have to come wherever she is. You had that bitch around my daughter when you know damn well she doesn't like me. I am so furious right now. I can't even look at you."

"Serenity, I fucked up, but you can't stop my daughter from coming over."

"Hakeem, I would never be that mother to keep a child from her father, but keep fucking playing with me, and I will show you a different side of me. You are too busy fucking that bitch that you almost made my daughter miss an important day of school. Take me back to Shay's. I can't do this with you."

She walked toward the car, and I followed her. She got in the back seat, and I shook my head. I knew things were going to change for the worst, and I had no one to blame but myself.

We pulled up to Shay's house, and she jumped out and slammed my door. I hated when females did that shit. I walked in the house behind her, and Shay was at the door.

"I take it he told you?" Shay asked her.

"You knew?" she asked.

"Yes. When you told me to go check on them, that's when I saw Rika. I told him he needed to tell you."

"So you fucking knew and didn't tell me, Shayla?"

"I didn't want to ruin your work day, and I felt it needed to come from him."

"I don't give a fuck where I was. My supposed to be best friend knew about the shit and didn't tell me. I would have told you right away."

"Serenity, she's right not to get in our business," I told her.

"You know what? Fuck the both of you."

She walked off and called for Naomi. Shay rolled her eyes at me and walked away. Serenity packed her things and headed for the door. I knew like hell she wasn't going to take my daughter out of the house.

"Where the fuck you going?" I asked.

"Don't fucking worry about it."

"Mommy, where are we going?" Naomi asked.

"Some place else, baby, but it'll be fun. Okay?"

"You're not about to do this. This shit is crazy. Why you taking my daughter through our bullshit? I told you I fucked up. It won't happen again."

"Oh, trust me. I know it won't."

She tried opening up the door, but I closed it back.

"Naomi go back in the room," I told her. She started to walk away, but Serenity pulled her back.

"We're leaving, Naomi."

"No, she's not."

I pulled Naomi's arm toward me, and Serenity pulled the other. She started cursing at me and yelling, and Naomi started crying. Seeing my baby cry fucked me up. I let her go and pushed Serenity back.

"You see what the fuck you're doing? You got my baby scared and confused."

"She wouldn't be confused if her father learned to think with his head and not his dick."

She pushed me, and Naomi cried more. I grabbed Serenity up and held her against the wall.

"Keep your fucking hands off me. It isn't about you. It's

about our daughter. At the end of the day, Rika is my girl, and if —"

Serenity had slapped the shit out of me. My reflex kicked in, and I had my hands around her neck.

"Daddy, no!" I heard Naomi scream, but it went on deaf ears. Shayla ran over and tried yanking my hands from around Serenity's neck.

"Let her go, Hakeem. Are you fucking crazy? You doing this shit in front of your daughter?"

I let her go, looked at Naomi, and walked away. I left and pulled off. I couldn't even comfort my baby girl, because I felt like shit.

I pulled into my mom's driveway, and I saw her peeking out the window. She opened the door, and I walked in.

"Are you okay, son?" she asked.

"I fucked up, mom, bad this time. I choked Serenity in front of Naomi."

"I know damn well you didn't say you choked that girl and in front of my grandbaby. What the hell is going on!" she yelled. I had never seen my mom so upset.

"Everything."

"You better give more details than that!"

I couldn't take her yelling at me.

"I brought Rika to the crib, and Serenity found out. We started arguing. I pushed her, and she pushed me, and I said some foul shit, so she slapped me, and I choked her."

"I am so disappointed in you. You had no right to put your hands on that girl. I don't care what the fuck she do."

"Look, I know it's foul. I'm just..."

I stopped talking because it was just too much for me. If I were a soft ass nigga, I would have been crying.

We sat down, and she started telling me stories about her childhood. She said her mother got beaten, and I could see why she felt concerned for Serenity, but I wasn't putting hands to her like that.

"I'm going to take Naomi to school and pick her up for a while. It's obvious you and Serenity need some space."

I didn't disagree with her on that. There was no way I could look at Serenity after that shit.

Serenity

It had been a month since the shit with Hakeem and I went down. It was June, and Naomi was out of school. We had a meeting with Naomi's teacher, and he didn't show. Instead, Denise, Hakeem's mom, attended. They talked about moving Naomi to the first grade, but Denise and I both agreed that we wanted to see how she did with Kindergarten first. If she was still advanced, we would pull her forward.

I had moved into my apartment and had everything set up. Shayla, Rashad, and Denise both helped. Shayla and I talked, and I had apologized to her the night everything happened. She understood why I was upset, and we forgave each other. Denise really started treating me different. She was nicer. She also picked Naomi up and drop her off for school, but now that Naomi was out for the summer, she kept her during the day or took her to Hakeem. I appreciated everything she did for us. Sacar and I really didn't get a chance to hang out as often as we would have liked, but we made do with whatever conversation we had. I only told Sacar a little about what happened between me and Hakeem. I didn't want to tell too much.

Everything was going good until Naomi started crying and asking for her daddy every day. I called Denise and asked if she could take her to see him. She told me no and that it was time Hakeem and I talked.

It was hours later when my doorbell rang, and Hakeem

was standing at my door. Naomi was in her room watching cartoons. I wanted to pretend as if he wasn't there, but I knew Naomi missed him. I opened the door, and he gave me a faint smile and spoke. It was hot as hell, so I knew he wanted to come in.

"Hey, it's hot out. Come in."

"Thanks, and yeah. It's like eighty-something degrees today. It feels like it's hotter."

Naomi, hearing her father's voice, ran into the living room and jumped into his arms.

"Hey, Daddy's princess," he said to her.

"Daddy, I really, really missed you."

"I missed you more. What have you been doing?"

"Playing with my toys and helping mommy," she said, giving him a silly grin. He chatted with her, and I walked away. It was Thursday, and I had Friday off. I was cooking dinner early because I wanted to relax and chill. I had only worked half a day, and I needed to get things around the house done.

"Food smells good," he said.

"Thanks."

"Daddy, can you stay to eat?" Naomi asked him.

"Umm, I don't know. Let's ask Mommy."

I wanted to slap his ass for saying that shit. If I said no, that would make me look like the bad person.

"It's enough to go around, so I guess."

Although a part of me wanted to hate him, I didn't want to come between him being in Naomi's life. If anything, he was an awesome dad.

Naomi cheered and pulled her daddy to her room. He looked at me, and I turned away, about ten minutes later he came out and walked into the kitchen. My little condo duplex was nice.

I had two bedrooms and a nice sized bathroom. The kitchen was big, and the dining area was an open concept attached to the living room.

"You got a nice lil spot here," he told me.

"Thanks."

"Serenity, we have to talk, and now is better than any other. Naomi is on her way to sleep. I told her to take a nap."

Naomi always listened to her father, so I believed him when he said she was on her way to sleep.

"I am so sorry for how things went down, and I'm especially sorry for putting my hands on you. I was foul, and it will never happen again."

"I really don't know what to say, but I guess I forgive you. It hurts most having my daughter see that shit."

"I know. I don't know what got into me, but you and Naomi mean the world to me, whether we're together or not. I just want you to know that I'm always here for you."

"Thanks. Great, Hakeem, and I appreciate it."

He got up and sat on the couch, and I wondered if he was still with Rika. I went to my room to get my phone and came back out. My question was answered when his phone rang, and he answered it.

"Sup, baby?" he asked. I walked over to the dining area to make my presence known.

"Aye, let me hit you back in a minute. I have to take care of something."

He ended his call, and I knew he hadn't change. He had disrespected me once again, and I was tired of it. I had the upper hand.

"My fault about that. I'm just trying to keep the peace," he stated.

"Well, peace up out of here. Every time I try to let shit go and move on, you do something else that's disrespectful. It's best that we not do this and continue to just have your mom bring Naomi back and forth to us."

"Serenity, Rika is my girl. I put her in her place about anything concerning my daughter. This is too much on Naomi, and it's confusing as hell."

"It's best."

"For who? You?"

"Yes, because my feelings and sanity matter as well. Just leave, Hakeem."

He got up and left. I shook my head because when Naomi woke up, she would have a fit that her daddy wasn't there to eat with her.

Hakeem

I didn't know why I always fucked up when it came to Serenity. I was just trying to keep the peace and make everyone happy. After she put me out, I called Rika to see what she was up to. She didn't answer, so I figured she was home. When I got there, her car wasn't there, so I pulled off and texted her to hit me up when she got home.

I was chilling with Rashad at the hub. He told me some shit he heard in the streets, and I just couldn't believe it.

"Man, nigga's saying Rika be out here on niggas."

"Man, niggas be hating and shit. You already know how the streets are. I'm not worried about Rika doing shit. Niggas just want what I got."

"Don't get me wrong, bro. Rika is fine, but I wouldn't fuck that hoe if she was the last bitch standing. She's a snake."

"Y'all just be bumping heads, and don't be calling my girl a hoe."

"Aight, man. I'll respect whatever y'all got going on. Anyway, on to other news. Have you heard anything about the niggas that was asking about us?" he asked.

"Hell nah. Dex didn't say shit. I got the crew on it as well. Pete ain't say shit else?" I asked him.

"Hell nah. I ain't heard from him."

"I'm thinking about opening up a few businesses. You already know moms doing her thing with opening a restaurant soon. I invested in that, but I really want to clean our money. Dex been schooling me on some shit. We got all this damn money and could be making more. I'm trying to have my money make money while I sleep."

"You already know I'm down. I got some shit I've been putting together too. We can most definitely get our hands in some shit."

"We got to, bro. This shit ain't guaranteed," I told him.

"You right about that. Let's sit down and talk business next week. Get whatever you have, and we'll collab, my nigga."

That's why I fucked with Rashad on business. He was always down. He wasn't just my day one nigga. He was more like a brother. He'd been down since the sandbox. His mother and father were both killed by gun violence, and my mom helped his granny raise him. He was deep in the game with me when his granny died.

"How's moms doing anyway?" he asked.

"Nigga, you asking that means you ain't been to see her. She gon' fuck you up, nigga."

"Shit, I want to introduce her to Shay."

"Shay? Nigga, she already knows Shay." I reminded his crazy ass.

"Not as my girl though."

"Yeah, you right about that."

After chatting, we decided to holla at the crew. I wanted to thank my team for working as hard as they did. I treated my team like family and made sure their pockets were fat.

We rode to a few spots, and Rashad just had to stop at the gas station to get a Sprite for the lean he had been drinking. I told him to stop fucking with that shit, but he was a grown ass man.

There were all types of hood niggas out there holding up the block. I wasn't worried about shit. Niggas knew who the fuck we were. I was sitting there, wondering why Rika hadn't called yet when I saw Rashad walking back to the car. I saw a chick walk up to him, and out of nowhere, gunshots rang through the air. I saw bodies hit the ground.

I started the car and grabbed my shit from underneath the seat. I saw Rashad crawl his way over to the car. I quickly opened the door for him and sped off. I asked if he was straight, and he was. I thought it was probably some young fools shooting at each other, but niggas knew when they saw my car not to do that shit around me. Hearing shots while driving, I knew they were directed at us. I was in my black Ferrari with the top down. Rashad said it was a black Hummer that was following us. I jumped on the highway and sped through traffic, turning and switching lanes until I lost whomever it was following.

I exited the highway and headed toward our spot. Rashad was on the phone with the crew. I called Dex, telling him I was going to find whoever it was, and when I did, I was going to fucking kill whoever it was. I hadn't gotten my hands dirty in a while, but I still had it.

"Put a price out there," I told one of my soldiers. I put $100,000 reward out there for whoever could give me information on who had been shooting at me and my boy. I was fucking seeing red and needed to calm down. It took a lot for me to get to the point where I wanted to off everyone walking.

"It's done, boss," Mohammad said. He was Japanese and Black. I had met him at the gun range and thought his aim was impressive. I approached him with a proposition to get money. At first, he acted as if he wasn't interested, but the more I talked about money, the more his curiosity stirred. The fact that he could shoot didn't mean that he was loyal, but I tested him a few times, and that nigga gained my trust. He was the leader of my soldiers. He kept them niggas in line. He always talked about keeping the trigger at a minimum, but he was the trigger-happy one. When we sent them to handle shit, someone always ended up dead.

I sat inside my office in the hub. I barely sat in there because I never wanted my team to feel I was superior to them. I wanted everyone to know we were a team and that their roles mattered. I laid my head back on the seat and closed my eyes. It wasn't the first time a nigga had come at me, but it was the first time of not knowing who the enemy was. I thought about everyone in my click and knew my team was solid. Then, I thought about Pete. He told us about some niggas asking about us. I found a few things wrong with that picture. He gave us that info, but for what? All I knew was that it was time for Killa Keem to surface and night a few niggas for good.

Rika

I lost my job and didn't really see the need to work. Between Hakeem and Moni, my account was loaded. I was chilling with Moni when Hakeem called. I put my phone on do not disturb. Moni said him and his boy, Sacar, had to handle street business, so I stayed at his crib and waited for him to return. I was happy he left because I needed to handle something anyway.

I sat on the side of the tub in Moni's bathroom, waiting for the results on the pregnancy test to appear. Sure enough, my ass was pregnant. I knew it was Moni's because he stayed fucking me raw. I couldn't get Hakeem to not put a condom on for the life of me. I had to weigh my options. I could tell Moni and be with him, but that meant Hakeem wouldn't be in my life, and as much as I really liked Moni, I was in love with Hakeem. I sat there, trying to decide on what I wanted to do. I thought about Hakeem and ran over to my phone. I had forgotten to turn it off do not disturb.

While I was about to call him, Moni walked in, so I laid the phone down. He walked over to me and started tonguing me down.

"I told you Daddy wasn't gon' make you wait long."

He walked over to his bathroom, and I had forgotten the pregnancy test on the sink. *Fuck,* I thought to myself. There was nothing I could do. When he went to wash his hands, he'd see it. When he walked out, I stared into his eyes. I didn't know if he'd be happy or mad.

"What's wrong, sexy?" he asked.

"I guess you know."

I held my head low.

"Know what?"

I thought about it and got disgusted. *This nigga didn't wash his damn hands,* I thought.

"Rika? What are you talking about?"

"That I wasn't satisfied earlier. I wanted you to make me cum all over your dick, and all you did was tease me."

"That's why you're pouting? You want Daddy to make you cum?"

I told him I needed to use the restroom first. Once I got in, I gathered the stuff and hid it until I could get rid of it later. We laid down, and I let him explore my body with his tongue.

It was way beyond midnight, and I hadn't called or reach out to Hakeem, but the excuse I would give him would make it believable. I told Moni I had to get home. He thought it was because I didn't want to be all clingy, so that's the excuse I gave him.

I got home and called Hakeem. He answered the phone and started going off on me. I smiled because baby was he mad.

"Hakeem, I had a long day, and I—"

I started crying, and he asked what was wrong.

"I'm pregnant."

"Pregnant!" he yelled out.

"Yes."

"How the fuck you get pregnant?"

"Hakeem, really?"

"Rika, I make sure I strap up every time so that shit like that won't happen."

"So you can have a baby with that bitch but not me?"

"Rika, have you even been to the doctor?"

"No. I took three pregnancy tests, and I lost my job today. I'm just fucking stressed out, and you're on the phone talking this shit to me. How the fuck you sound?"

"Look, I'm handling some shit right now. When I get done, I'll come through. Don't even worry about it, but we have to talk about this pregnancy thing."

Pregnancy thing, I thought. I had to play my cards right. I couldn't wait until I could rub my pregnancy in Serenity's ugly face.

Rashad

"I can't believe someone shot at you," Shay said.

"I know, baby, but when I find out who it is, it's lights out for them niggas."

"I hate that you're caught up in this street shit. There is so much more you can be doing."

"Baby, please don't go there this early."

It was Friday morning, and I had all type of shit to do. I laid in my bed with Shay, and she was so worried about me. She knew the life I lived, but she also knew the savage I was. She got up and made a nigga breakfast before she headed to work. I loved that she was so independent and ambitious. Everything about her screamed *boss.*

I walked down my gold and bronze staircase to head into the kitchen. I looked up at the show-stopping chandelier and admired my house. A home was where you felt most at peace, and I wanted Shay to move in, but I knew we needed to build on that. She wasn't the type of girl to jump into something so quickly.

"You got it smelling right up in here, sexy," I told her. She smiled and poured up orange juice for me. My plate was already waiting on the granite countertop of the island inside my kitchen. I sat my phone on the counter and bit into the bacon. She looked at me and smiled.

"I'm cooking the last of the bacon, and that's it, Rashad.

You said you doing this no pork thing, but you got bacon all throughout the fridge."

"I know, baby, and I'm working on it. It's hard switching your diet up, but your man fine as fuck, ma. You can't complain."

"The outside isn't what's important, but I have to get ready for work. Thank God it's Friday," she sang as she tried walking off. I grabbed her before she walked by and pulled her close to me. I kissed her lips and tongued her down. My arms were around her waist, and all she wore were her panties and my T-shirt. I pulled her between my legs and started rubbing her ass.

"Rashad, we did that all night now. I have to go and get ready."

"You got enough time to take care of your man," I said, sucking on her neck. She moaned and pulled away.

"Later, baby. I promise."

She took off, and I laughed. I was sure to punish the pussy later. My phone started to vibrate next to me, and it was Pete. I answered and listened.

"I got some info for you and Keem," he told me.

"Oh, yeah? What kind of info?"

"Info that will land $100,000 in my lap."

"Say less. I'll call you in a minute, and we'll meet up."

I called Hakeem, and he didn't answer. I shook my head because he was fucking up lately and a little more than usual the past few days. My phone vibrated, and it was him calling back.

"The hub in an hour."

I hung up and continued to eat. We didn't do that phone shit when it came to the streets. I ate and showered. Shay was already gone when I got out. She made the bed and organized the room for a nigga before she left.

Sitting inside of Keem's office inside the hub, he stared at me. I knew the same shit was on his mind that was on mine. I told him about Pete having information for us.

"What you think?" he asked.

"Hard to say, but being that there's a reward involved, he's probably ready to sell his soul."

"I don't know. Something about him calling to give us information ain't sitting well with me, but let's go meet up with this nigga. If the information is valuable, we'll pay him. Get the crew to get the money together, and let's roll."

We headed to a warehouse downtown in the city on the rough side of town. It was a spot we met up with many cats that we chatted with or took care of, meaning we offed their asses.

"I'm going back and forth with my thoughts right now about how the shit is going to go down. I just pray he came at us correct, or it's over for his ass. I don't trust Pete. That's why he always called yo' ass with the shit he heard from the street," Keem said as tore the streets up, flying in his Ferrari. Everything he did had meaning behind it.

We pulled up and drove through the alley. The warehouse was in a secluded area where no one lived. I got out and grabbed the bag from the back. If Pete disclosed any useful information, the money was his. Keem and I were men of our word.

We scoped the area out, and our crew wasn't too far behind. We weren't stupid. We had eyes on us. A car pulled in, and Pete quickly jumped out. That was another thing Keem didn't like about him. He was a show off. He always wanted attention.

"Sup?" he said, walking over to us. I spoke and gave him some dap. Keem walked away, heading into the warehouse. Once we got in and secured the door so that no one else could come in, I looked at Pete as to say *speak*.

"I have the info. Y'all got the money?" he asked.

"Of course. What's the information?" Keem asked.

"When I say this shit, I don't want no pressure coming back down on me. I'm just delivering what I know."

"We got you, homie," I told him. I saw how impatient Hakeem was getting, and I prayed he didn't pull his gun out and just shoot him.

Hakeem

My patience was thin when it came to hearing niggas out. I didn't like or really fuck with Pete. Being that he was cool with Rashad, I gave his ass some leeway. I stood there, waiting on the nigga to talk, but he was fucking playing with me. He had one time to fuck up, and I was going to put a bullet between his eyes.

"Remember when I said some niggas were asking about y'all in the streets? Well them same niggas were shooting at y'all. From what I know, no one saw who it was because mothafuckers were too busy running and ducking from the gunshots. One nigga said that they were shooting at a black truck. No one knows exactly who they were shooting at. I didn't hear shit about y'all even being there. They mentioned that Rashad came in the store, but they didn't even say you were there, Hakeem. However, the niggas are from Baltimore. They're trying to come up on a lick and take over your territory.

Keep talking, you dumb mothafucker. Dig that grave for your-self, I thought to myself.

"The niggas names are Sacar and Moni, from what I know."

"Never heard of them," Rashad voiced.

"Yeah, me either, but like I said, they're from Baltimore."

I looked at Rashad and threw Pete the bag of money.

"Pete, how you be knowing all the info?" I asked.

"Shit, man. Resources... that's all."

I shook my head and told him I appreciated him giving us the information. We headed out. Rashad was in front of me, and Pete walked behind me.

"It's good them niggas didn't hit your Ferrari though, because that bitch too nice to be taking a beating," he said.

"How the hell you know that I was in my Ferrari when you said your resource didn't even know I was there?" I asked.

"Oh, you know my... my other resources told me."

I pulled my gun out and turned around to him. He stopped, and at that moment, he knew he had fucked up.

"Your resources seem fraud," I said, letting off a bullet. It hit him right between the eyes where I wanted it to go.

"Damn, I didn't see that coming. Warn a nigga next time," Rashad insisted.

"Didn't have time to, but he exposed himself by talking too damn much. I wasn't letting that nigga leave this warehouse.

"Damn, Pete. You was a good nigga, knew all the gossip of the streets, and now you're a dead nigga. Oh well. Lose my number, nigga."

I chuckled and looked at Rashad.

"Did you just tell a dead nigga to lose your number?" I asked.

"Hell yeah. Nigga ain't about to ghost call me throughout the night."

"Man, come the fuck on. I can't take your ass nowhere."

"You gon' leave the money, fool?"

"Yes. Like I always say, I'm a man of my word. He gave us the info, so it's his money."

"Nigga, you crazy," he expressed, walking off with the bag of money. I couldn't help but laugh while walking to the car. The crew took Pete's car. It was an entry level Benz, but he acted as if it was one of them big boys.

As we drove down the highway, Rashad started laughing. I looked over at him and asked what was funny.

"Your aim has improved. You shot the nigga exactly five centimeters from his eyes."

"Man, I can't wait to drop your ass off to Shay."

Even though we laughed and joked, there was still a matter at hand. Sacar and Moni had asked about us. Now they had us, but what I had for them, I knew they didn't want it. We just had to find out who they were.

"Aye, you get things straight with Serenity yet?"

"Nope. I'm done. It's like we take two steps forward and then ten steps back. It's my fault though. I keep fucking up."

"Man, on the real, I don't know why you won't just get your family back. You been my boy for damn near my whole life. What's really good?"

"Truth? I love Serenity. I don't think she respects me though. It's like she has something to prove to me. It's like she wants to say she don't need me for shit. I know I fucked up a few times by throwing shit in her face about what I did for her. Honestly, I don't think I know how to love for real. Shit, I barely make time for Rika's ass, and do you know the bitch claiming she's pregnant by me?"

"Nigga, come again?"

"Exactly! I see what you're saying. I just need to play my cards right and do what I need to do."

"I can't believe you entertaining this shit, man."

"Just know I'm doing it because I want to. Besides, she got that lethal head game."

"It's lethal alright, more like suicidal."

"Man, stop."

I laughed and focused on the road. I dropped Rashad off to Shay's, and I noticed Serenity was there. I wanted to see Naomi, so I went in.

"Sup, sis?" I asked Shay, walking into her living room with Rashad. He tongued her down, and I looked away at Serenity sitting on the sofa. She was looking bad as fuck in her jeans, blouse, and heels. I subconsciously licked my lips, and she turned away.

"Where is my baby?" I asked Serenity.

"She right there, ain't she?" Rashad teased. I glared at him, and he smirked.

"She's at your mom's for the weekend. She wants to take her for swimming lessons," Serenity revealed.

"Oh, hell nah. Y'all didn't ask me. My baby can't swim."

"That's why it's swimming lessons, nigga, not a swim tournament," Shay stated.

"Shay, don't start with me."

"I'm not starting shit. You lucky I even let you in my house."

"Yeah, whatever. I'm about to be out. What y'all about to get into?" I asked to no one in particular.

"Well, Serenity is going on a date, and Rashad and I are going to dinner. How about yourself?"

I looked at Serenity, and she wouldn't look my way. I wanted to question her, but I knew I had no right to. It was hard as hell to walk away and not say shit.

"I'm out. I'll holla at y'all later."

"Aye, you straight, homie?" Rashad asked as I walked outside of the door.

"Yeah, why you asked that?"

"I'm just asking, bro, but you're letting her slip further and further away. You better get your girl, bro."

"You funny, but I know she's going to tell Shay about the date, so let me know what's up."

"Man, get your tender dick ass on," he said, laughing.

"Don't tell her about the shooting nigga. I know you told Shay already."

"Shay won't say shit, man, but she's worried you'll have Naomi in the car with you one day and some shit will pop off."

"Nah, I'll be more cautious next time. I'll paint this city red if someone do some shit like that with my baby in the car."

He agreed. I gave him a brotherly hug and jumped in my ride to head over Rika's crib. A nigga had a baby on the way.

Serenity

"Y ou're so damn beautiful, Serenity. I could look at you all day," Sacar told me.

"Thank you. You're quite handsome yourself."

Sacar invited me over for dinner, and I accepted the offer. I hadn't seen and barely talked to him in weeks. He took all my stress and pain away. The candle light dinner and set-up on his patio was just the right gesture I needed from him. The warm breeze wasn't as pleasant, but it was manageable. He had a lovely home, and I knew he ran the streets like Hakeem. It wasn't hard to figure out. I asked Shay to switch cars with me so that I wouldn't have to take Hakeem's car.

"How was your day? Did you enjoy your day off?" he asked.

"I did. It was nice to have a day to just get things in order around my place. I still had boxes to put away, so I got that done. Naomi's granny stopped by and asked to take her for the weekend. At first, I declined because I thought she was over there enough, especially throughout the week when I was working."

"You deserve a break, baby. There's nothing wrong with letting others help you out."

"I know, and I'm learning that. I was just used to people throwing what they did for me in my face."

He stared at me and smiled.

"Are you referring to your baby daddy?" he asked. I didn't want to get into talking about my baby daddy, but I felt I could trust him.

"Yes, but it is what it is."

"I don't like how that nigga be stressing my girl out," he expressed.

"Your girl?" I questioned him.

"Yes, my girl. I'm trying to make it official with you."

"Well, I'm trying to let you."

I was cheesing from ear to ear. I needed him in my life, and I prayed Hakeem didn't run him off. I told him the relationship Hakeem and I had and how I had stayed with him. He damn near choked when I said that.

"He never tried coming on to you?"

"No," I lied. I couldn't tell him we had fucked, and recently at that.

"Damn, I can't see how he didn't, but what made you stay with him knowing he had a girl?"

"It was convenient, and like I said, I didn't really have anywhere else to go. Naomi played a major part in it as well. He wanted her to live with him, but he was controlling at times."

"Are you ready for dessert?" he asked, changing the subject.

"What did you make?"

"Nothing. I'm talking about me."

I instantly got hot and bothered. It wasn't like I didn't want him. We were both grown. I just didn't want to go in that direction just yet.

"I'm not really ready for that. I'm sorry."

"No need to apologize. When you're ready for me, I'll come

running with my dick swinging."

I laughed so hard that I started to choke on my wine he had poured up for me. We retired to his living room and laid down to cuddle on the couch. He said he wanted to experience the whole Netflix and cuddle thing. I told him it wasn't what it was all hyped up to be.

Sacar had to take a call, so he stepped away. I was laughing at the movie *Girls Trip* when Hakeem texted me, asking to come switch cars with him. I laughed because for the first time, I didn't have his car, and I didn't have to stop what I was doing.

Me: The car is at Shay's

Naomi's Dad: How the fuck you getting around.

Me: Not your business, Gn!

Naomi's Dad: That's how you doing it now?

I didn't text him back, because I wasn't about to text back and forth with his crazy ass. Sacar came back from taking his call.

"My fault, baby."

He cuddled back up with me and asked me to spend the night. I looked up at him and told him I would.

Sacar and I stayed up all night talking. I showed him pictures of Naomi again, and he said she looked like me. Everyone else said she looked like her dad, although she did look a little like me. I rubbed his face, and he kissed me. He was so crazy. He had his hands behind his head because he said he was gon' touch me in places he didn't need to. After a while, we stopped kissing, because it was getting intense. He had fallen asleep, and his phone started vibrating. It was on his side of the bed. I didn't know whether to wake him up or let him sleep. I just decided to lie down and let him deal with it when he woke up. I just hoped he wasn't missing anything important.

∞∞∞∞

I woke up to my alarm clock going off on my phone. I had forgotten to turn it off. Yeah, I had an alarm clock to go off on Saturday mornings. It was my only time to get peace before the brat woke up. I looked around and Sacar was nowhere in the room. I got up and entered his bathroom. It was so spacious. On the counter, he had left a toothbrush, face towel, and bath towel out for me. I looked in the bag on the floor, and there was a sundress with a panty and bra set inside. I smiled because he was just too much. My day had started just great.

I showered and did my hair. I put the dress on he had got me and walked down stairs.

When I got to the bottom of the stairs, I saw him in the kitchen moving around like he owned it. I stared at him shirtless and thought about him being in between my legs. I hadn't had sex with anyone but Hakeem, so I wondered if it would be better. That was the issue of having sex with him. All I knew was Hakeem.

"Damn, you're so beautiful," he said, staring at me. I was too busy daydreaming that I didn't even notice he was looking at me. I walked into the kitchen, and he greeted me.

"Good morning, sexy."

"Good morning, and thank you for the dress. I really love the colors."

It was a coral and grey. It stopped just before my knees and fit just right. I knew once I stepped out in public, niggas would be hollering they loved sundress season.

"I thought you would."

"When did you go out and buy this, and where? It's 8:00 in the morning."

"Don't question your man. Just be sexy, and flaunt it for me."

"You're so crazy, and you're cooking again? You got me spoiled. I could have made you breakfast."

"Oh, you'll get your chance, but I want to take care of you. You deserve it, baby."

I sat down on the stool and waited for the food to be done. Once he was finished, he made our plates, said grace, and we ate.

"I have to take care of a few things today, baby. You can stay here. I won't be out long."

"No, it's okay. I have to check on Naomi anyway. That brat is a handful sometimes."

"I wonder where she gets it from."

"You know... I don't know."

After we ate, he got dressed, and we both left at the same time. I called Denise, and she said Naomi was still sleep. She had let her stay up all night. I shook my head because Naomi always got over on them. I called Shay to see if she was up for a mani and pedi. She said she was, and I went to pick her up.

"Bitch, I needed my feet done. Rashad keep cracking on my feet."

She laughed, and I smiled. They were so cute together, and I knew she was happy because she had been glowing a lot lately.

"So how was your night?" she asked.

"It was nice. He bought me this dress and the panty and bra set I'm wearing."

"Bitch, you put it on him good, didn't you? Did he wake up and make you breakfast?"

"He did, but I didn't sleep with him."

"Girl, I already knew that. I just wanted you to say it. Besides... Hakeem was your one and only."

"What is that supposed to mean?"

"That Hakeem got your pussy shaped to fit around his dick. You're custom to his shit."

"Really, Shay, I am not. I mean, just because he was my first doesn't mean anything."

"Your first and only? Yeah, that means nothing, but anyway… subject changed."

"No, let's have this talk. So you think because I haven't given it up that I'm stuck on Hakeem's dick as you put it?"

"Yes."

"Okay, we shall see."

"See what? Wait a minute. I was just playing. Don't you go out there and get dicked down. Hakeem's ass gon' be waiting in a closet. As soon as Sacar pull his dick out, Hakeem gon' jump out and chop it off."

"Where do you get this shit from? I swear your ass needs to write a book or something."

"I'm just saying. Don't jump into anything because of what's going on now. You never know. You and Hakeem may get back together."

"What the hell? Are you the Shay I know? It can't be, because she wouldn't say no shit like that."

"I'm just saying. You never know."

"Lord, did Rashad brainwash you or something?"

"No, but I know that Hakeem still loves you."

"Okay, subject change please."

I didn't know what she was on, but she needed to get off fast and not slow. After we were pampered, we headed to the mall. We needed some retail therapy. I bought Naomi a few things and got the rest of her stuff with Hakeem's black card. I had picked up a shirt from H&M for him and put it back down. I didn't know why I was even looking for him something. It was a habit I needed to break. When I was staying with him, he would have me look for something for him when I was out shopping. Being that it was his money, I had no problem doing it.

I looked over at Shay, taking a pic. She was looking too cute in her romper short set. I walked over and got in her picture with her. I moved my hair back, and she held the camera up, only to quickly take it back down.

"Uh oh!"

"What?"

I looked at her as if she was crazy. She turned me around to the full mirror and pointed at something on my neck. I walked closer to the mirror, and it was a passion mark. I laughed because she acted like I was going to get in trouble.

"Girl, you act like it was something serious. Don't be scaring me like that."

"Hakeem gon' beat your ass," she uttered.

"He can't do shit to me. I'm not his girl."

"Yep, okay. Do not come over my house today. I ain't trying to see that ass whooping."

I couldn't do shit but laugh. My friend was too damn funny for me to deal with.

Hakeem

Rashad was outside, waiting on me to come out of Rika's house. I knew he was probably pissed sitting out there in the car. I never came to see her last night. She was pissed and threatening a nigga, so I had to calm her little ass down.

"First of all, you're pregnant, and you don't want to stress the baby."

"Hakeem, you're the one stressing me the fuck out. You said you were coming last night. What happened?"

"I got into some shit in the streets, but I apologize for not showing, sexy. You forgive me?" I asked her.

"I guess."

She walked over and kissed my lips. I stared at her as she closed her eyes and kissed me. I pulled away and told her I had to go.

"Rashad out there in the car."

"What?"

"We got some shit to handle today, baby."

"Hakeem, all I wanted to do was talk to you about everything I've been going through, losing my job, and the pregnancy. I just want to know that my baby's daddy is gon' be there for me."

"I'm sure he will be."

I smiled and kissed her forehead. I gave her a stack, and she instantly smiled. I jumped inside of my Bentley. It was parked at Shay's house, and when I came to scoop Rashad, I decided to just drive it. I parked my Ferrari in the back of her house. I didn't need anyone messing with my shit.

"Man, your ass is crazy, fool," Rashad said.

"Hey, the game isn't fair. All I can do is play my hand."

"Whatever, but if you ain't doing shit later on, Shay and Serenity having drinks over Shay's house. You might as well come chill and have a drink with ya boy."

"Nigga, I ain't trying to be all in that girl's face."

"Yeah, whatever. You wanna know what time?"

"Yeah, what time?"

He laughed, and I burst out laughing too.

"How many times have y'all fucked now?" he asked.

"Only two, but if I get lucky, maybe it'll be three tonight."

"You be raw dogging her, don't you?"

"Hell yeah. That's the only pussy I'll run up in. I'm the only one been up in that."

"How long do you think it will stay that way?"

"Why you always do that shit… ruin my moment?" I asked as I pulled up to my mom's crib. When I walked in, Naomi was at the counter, eating and watching TV. I laughed because when she saw me, she screamed.

"Hey, princess."

"Hey, Daddy. Hey, Uncle Ra-Ra."

"Hey, lil' mama. What you eating?"

"Oatmeal," she said excitedly.

"So my son has to kidnap you so that I can see you?" my mom asked, hugging Rashad.

"Aww, ma. It ain't even like that. You know I love you. I just been busy with work."

"Y'all gon' quit calling what y'all do work."

We laughed and headed into the living room. I asked where Coli was, and she said he was at the restaurant they were opening. I couldn't wait to eat my mom's cooking every day.

"Ma, you know Rashad got a girlfriend?"

I busted him out.

"And I haven't met her yet?"

"You have, but I'll reintroduce her as my girl."

"Who is she?"

"You'll see."

"Lord, I hope it ain't none of them fast lil' heifers."

"Nah, you'll like her. I promise."

"I better because if she's anything like Rika, I'm going to kick your ass."

Rashad laughed so hard, and I didn't see what was so funny.

"Ma, you do the most."

"I'm just saying. You should be trying to get Serenity back and get your family back together."

"So when did everyone become team Serenity all of a sudden?"

"We been team Serenity," Rashad voiced.

"Nah, moms used to complain about her not doing this and not doing that."

"That was then. This is now. You keep playing, and Naomi gon' be calling someone else Daddy."

"Over my dead body."

"Y'all know she be eavesdropping. She gon' tell Serenity everything," Mom stated.

"Don't I know it," I stated, getting up. I cleaned Naomi up after I saw she was done eating. I answered her fifty questions before she let me get a question in.

"How was swimming? I asked her.

"It was fun. I can swim now, Daddy."

"You can? Well, I'll have to buy you a swimming pool now."

"Yes, you do, and when you buy it, can you buy me a new bike?"

"A new bike? Didn't you just get a new bike last year?"

"I was three. I'm four now."

I didn't even argue with the princess. I just told her what she wanted to hear.

"Yeah, I'll get you another bike."

"Can I get a horse too?"

Rashad burst out laughing. I couldn't hide my laughs either.

"You know I don't do animals, baby."

"Uncle Ra-Ra, can you buy me a horse?"

"I sure can, but you'll have to keep it at the stadium, and we'll go visit every so often."

"Yay! Uncle Ra-Ra, you're the best."

She looked at me and gave me a fake smile.

"Go watch TV, princess."

She took off running, and I shook my head.

"Let's roll, nigga."

After we left, we went to the hub. I pulled the crew in and asked about them niggas Sacar and Moni. No one knew them, but we would eventually find out who they were.

I called Dex, and he said he was working on getting us visuals of them niggas. I told him about Pete, and he wasn't surprised.

It was getting dark when we pulled up to Shay's crib. I had gotten a few drinks because I didn't fuck with wine like that to be sipping on it all night. When we got in, Shay had music playing, and they were laughing about something. When Serenity saw me, her eyes got big.

"I hope you didn't mind me taking the Bentley."

"It's yours. Why would I mind?"

Hope she doesn't start acting stank, I thought to myself. I poured up some Hennessy on ice. Rashad had Vodka, and the girls had their wine. We played cards, and Shay wanted to be on Rashad's team while playing spades. Therefore, it was us against them.

I looked at Serenity sitting across from me. She was looking so damn sexy. She wore a pair of lounge pants and a top. Her hair was hanging down with curls, and her lips were looking like she needed my kisses. I just pictured my nut hanging from her lips.

"Hakeem?" Serenity called out to me.

"Oh, my fault. What's up?"

"How many books do you have?"

"I got three."

"Okay, I got about six," she told us. Throughout the game, Shay would say sorry for bumping Serenity's foot under the table. I took that as the opportunity to play footsie with her.

"Shay, get your feet off me," Serenity said, laughing.

"Friend, that's not me this time."

"Damn, my bad," I told her, only I started doing it again

after a while. She glanced up at me, and I winked at her. She pulled her hair back, and I could not believe my eyes.

"I know that's not a hickey on your damn neck, is it?" I asked her. It got quiet, and all of a sudden, Rashad and Shay started laughing. Serenity looked away, and I decided to let the shit go. I was semi-lit and needed to stay calm. I wanted to yank her lil' ass up about that shit.

"What y'all about to do? Me and bae about to go in the room and fuck," Shay said. I looked over at Serenity, and she was looking at her phone smiling.

"What's funny? Care to share?"

"Nope."

She got up and told Shay she was leaving, but I wasn't about to let her drive knowing she had been drinking.

"Hakeem, give me my keys."

"You been drinking, Serenity. Just stay here, and sleep it off."

"Hell nah. I'm not about to listen to them fuck like rabbits all night."

I laughed, and she joined in. I hadn't seen her smile like that in a while.

"I'll drop you off at home."

"I'm okay to drive, Hakeem."

"Nah, I can't risk something happening to you. Naomi would be devastated."

"Okay, I guess, but I'm really not that drunk."

We locked up and headed to her condo. The drive over was quiet. We talked about Naomi and her schooling. Once we pulled up, I walked her to the door.

"Thanks, Hakeem. You really didn't have to go out of your way to bring me home."

"I told you that it's cool. Can I use the restroom?" I asked.

"Oh, yeah. Of course. She unlocked her door and pointed to where it was. I noticed that the boxes that were on the floor last time were gone. I assumed she had gotten everything unpacked and put away. There was a nice vanilla smell. She loved candles, so I knew she would have them everywhere.

When I came out the bathroom, she was sitting on the couch. I walked up behind her and gently pulled her hair back. I looked at the mark left on her neck.

"So you letting other niggas suck on you?"

"Hakeem, please don't start."

"Can we talk, like really just have a long talk about everything, and I need to tell you about some other shit."

"How long is this going to take?" she asked.

"Not sure. It depends on how the conversation goes."

She didn't respond, and I took that as a yes.

"Serenity, no matter how hard I try to not love you, I do. I'm sorry once again for everything that happened between us. Seeing you smile today was like an eye opener because I haven't made you smile in a very long time. I don't want you to hate me."

"I don't hate you, Hakeem. I just hate the choices you make. It's like you can do whatever you want, but when it comes to me, it's a problem. Rika should have never been in your home that day while Naomi was there."

Just sitting there thinking about it, I knew she was right. I wasn't thinking or putting Naomi first.

"I love you, Serenity. I want my family back."

I sat next to her on the couch.

"Hakeem, I love you too, and we're still family. Our living arrangements are just different."

"I don't think you understand what I'm saying. I want us

144

to be together and raise our daughter together."

Serenity

I couldn't believe we were even having the conversation about being together, after everything he had done to me.

"Hakeem, I don't think we're meant to be together. I'm seeing someone right now, and so are you."

"Serenity, if you told me that we could start over, it would only be me and you."

"I can't believe we're having this discussion right now."

"I know you said you ended things with me because I was too controlling, but I just wanted to protect you and Naomi. I'm still in love with you. I love everything about you. I want to hear of your accomplishments. It hurt when you didn't tell me you were in school. When you're having a bad day, I want to make it better. Do you know how happy Naomi would be if we stayed together as a family and you and I slept in the same bed? I miss your touch and your kisses. I can't stand to think of you kissing another nigga."

"How you think I felt when you fucked me and then I saw Rika coming out of your room the very next day?"

"I know, and I was foul about that. I fucked up. Honestly, I thought we just had a weak moment."

"Hakeem, this is crazy. Even though I love you, I just feel like it's not going to work out."

"It will if we both try hard enough."

He got closer, and I knew he was going to try it. He tried to kiss me.

"Hakeem, don't."

"I want you."

"And then what? Tomorrow, you'll be with her?"

"No. Tomorrow, I'll be with you like I am now."

He kissed my neck, and I couldn't help but compare his kisses to Sacar's. Sacar kisses were nice, and he turned me on, but Hakeem always made my body quiver with just the touch of his lips.

"I love you, baby. Give me the chance to be that man for you."

The tears emerged from my eyes, and I closed them to let whatever was going to happen, happen. He turned my head to face his, and he kissed me. Our tongues wrestled with one another, and then he stopped. He rose from the couch and pulled me up. He directed me toward my bedroom. I wasn't surprised about him knowing where it was, because he always paid close attention to his surroundings.

As Hakeem stroked in and out of me, I held his hands tightly. I forgot all about the pain he had caused me and just enjoyed whatever we had at the moment, even if it was for one night. I felt our love was convenient. Maybe I loved him because I felt I had to for our daughter, and maybe he felt the same.

"I love you, baby," he told me.

"I love you too."

∞∞∞

The next morning, I woke up and felt like I was being held

down. I looked down, and Hakeem had me wrapped in his arms. The position was awkward because he had all of his weight on me. I couldn't even move. I thought about everything he said and still didn't know how to feel.

"Hakeem. Hakeem," I said, shaking him. He opened his eyes and smiled. I couldn't help but smile as well.

"I can't breathe. Get your ass off me."

"My fault, baby. I had to make sure you weren't going to disappear in the middle of the night."

"Ha."

I got up and walked into my bathroom. I looked into the mirror and wondered what was going to come of us. Hakeem walked in and wrapped his arms around my waist. He kissed the back of my neck and asked how I was feeling.

"I'm okay. I'm just unsure of my feelings right now."

"The last thing I want is for you to be unsure. I'll give you some space to think everything over. If you then say that you don't want to be with me, I'll respect that."

"I think space will help a lot."

I didn't want to push him away, but I needed space.

"I have something else to tell you," he confessed.

"Okay."

"Rashad and I got shot at a few days ago."

"What?"

I turned around, looking at him.

"I'm okay, as you can see. From what I heard, it was some niggas up here from Baltimore trying to take over. They want my spot, but I'll be damned if I go down without a fight. We already got the names. We just waiting on some visuals."

"Hakeem, what if Naomi was in the car with you?"

"I know. I keep thinking the same thing, but my team working on finding them niggas."

"I know you can handle yourself out there, and everyone knows how you get down, but that still don't make you invincible,"

"I know, Serenity. I'll be careful."

"I think it's best if Naomi doesn't ride with you. How did they know where to find you?"

"Niggas talking, but I don't want you worrying about that. I won't bring any harm to my family. That's for sure. I won't have Naomi in the car with me if that makes you feel better."

"It does."

"I have to meet the crew in a few hours to handle some shit. You know I don't usually tell you stuff for your safety, but I wanted you to know," he said, pulling his shirt over his head. I just looked at him and prayed in my head.

"So now what?" I asked.

"What you mean?"

"With us. What happens?"

"We build that trust back. We can't let anyone come between us. Rika may be a problem, but I can handle her."

"What you mean a problem?"

"I just know she ain't going to take it lightly. She hates you, and she already thought we'd been fucking around."

"This guy I'm seeing, I really like him. If you're just stringing me along so that you can have your cake and eat it too, just please leave me alone, Hakeem."

He looked at me as if his feelings were hurt, but he cared for someone. Why couldn't I?

"Get dressed," he said, leaving the bathroom.

"Why?"

"I drove you home last night. You have to drop me back off to Shay's to get my car."

"Oh yeah. Give me a minute."

I stared in the mirror again. *Am I really doing this*?

Shayla

Rashad and I were on our way to Denise's house. I had already met Denise, so I didn't know why I had to meet her again. Rashad said he wanted to introduce me as his girlfriend. Denise was making a big dinner, so I didn't decline. She was the best cook in Texas if you asked me. I couldn't wait until she opened her restaurant.

Once we made it in, Serenity was at the table with Naomi coloring. Naomi had on a cute little sundress, looking like the doll she was. Once she saw me, her eyes got as big as saucers.

"God mommy."

She leaped from her chair over to me as I got close.

"Hey, baby. You look so pretty, and look at this hair."

Naomi's hair was in a ponytail, looking fluffy and cute. She had long pretty hair, so to see it puffy and curly looked pretty on her.

"God mommy, guess what?" she asked.

"What, princess?"

She whispered in my ear, and I burst out laughing. If she wasn't the cutest child I'd ever met! I put her down and sat at the table with Serenity. Rashad had walked off to find Denise.

"Why haven't I seen my best friend? I know you saw my text last night?"

"I did, but I was busy."

"Doing?"

She never answered because Rashad, Denise, and Coli walked in. I stood up to hug Denise, and she looked somewhat confused.

"Ma, this my girl, Shayla," Rashad told her.

"Oh my God, Shay. You know I thought this boy had some lil' trick coming up in here. I'm so happy it's you, and I knew y'all liked each other last time we were at Hakeem's house. Y'all didn't think I saw when he sucked the barbeque off your finger. I said to myself, yeah… they fucking tonight."

We all burst out laughing. I hugged her and Coli. Hakeem walked in, and everyone got quiet.

"What? Y'all talking about a boss, ain't y'all?" he asked.

"Nah, ain't nobody thinking about you," Denise said as she walked over and kissed his cheek.

"I'll have the food out in a bit. You men can go out back until it's ready," she told them before walking off.

"Sup with y'all?" Keem asked.

"Nothing much. What's up with you, bro?"

"Man, I'm tired as hell. I been up all night," he stated.

"Oh yeah? What you been up doing?"

He looked at Serenity and smiled before walking off. I stared at her because something was off about them. They were getting along and not talking shit to one another. I knew she had to have fucked him the night she left my house, but I didn't think they'd been doing it on the regular.

"Hello?" Serenity said, answering her phone.

"Hey, I'm actually at a dinner right now. I'll call you later. Okay, and I know."

She hung up, and I asked who she was talking to when Hakeem walked up on her from behind. He snatched her phone from her hand and glared down at her.

"My boo?" he read.

"I thought you got rid of that nigga," he snapped.

"I never said that, but can we talk later?" she stated. Hakeem handed her phone back to her, and I stared between the two. I had so many questions, but I didn't ask.

We sat around the dinner table, eating and talking. Denise was so funny. She kept putting Hakeem and Rashad on blast about their line of work.

"So Serenity, how are you liking the job?" Denise asked.

"I love it. I was a little timid at first, working in a prison, but it's really not how everyone thinks."

"That's awesome. I'm proud of you. I know I haven't said that to you, so I just wanted you to know."

"Thank you."

I was half listening because Rashad kept rubbing between my thighs at the dinner table. I tried my best to pull his hand away. He smiled, licked his lips, and finally took a sip of his lemonade.

"What did Naomi whisper in your ear when you first got here?" Serenity asked me.

"That child is too funny. She said Uncle Ra-Ra likes you."

"Lord, I tell you that child has been here before," Denise told us. We all laughed and continued eating our food. Afterwards, the guys joined Coli in the great room while we women cleaned the kitchen. Naomi was in her room inside her granny's house.

"Are you and my son back together?" Denise asked. Denise was a very beautiful woman. Hakeem looked just like her, which was why I always said Naomi looked like her granny.

"No, we're not. What made you ask that?" Serenity asked as she wiped down the island's granite countertop. The kitchen décor was amazing. I just found myself looking around at the high ceiling lights.

"I don't know. I just sensed something strange between you two."

"He wants to get back together," Serenity confessed. I all of the sudden got hot. The cool air from the central air inside the house did nothing for me. I knew Hakeem had told Rashad he wanted him and Serenity to work things out and be together, but I didn't know he had asked her. I was so excited. I wanted to ask so many questions. I was getting anxious.

"So what's the problem? Why aren't you guys together? You two have a beautiful daughter together. I know my son is a lot to deal with and can be hot headed at times, but he's a good man. He just needs someone who will put him in his place when he's wrong and someone who will be there for those stressful nights. He needs a woman, and Serenity, I see that woman in you. At first, I must admit that I didn't approve of y'all relationship and living arrangement, but now I finally see why he wanted to keep you close. That man loves you, and he's not going to stop until he has you. Now I know all about the Rika chick, but honey, she has nothing on you. Believe me when I tell you that. You have the upper hand," Denise expressed.

"How? Because I have a child with him?" Serenity asked. I wanted to know the answer as well.

"Because you have his heart."

"I don't know about all of that. Yes, he did a lot for me, but we slept together few times recently, and he's still with Rika. I'm seeing someone else as well, and I really like him."

"Wait a minute. You're both seeing other people and still sleeping together?" Denise examined.

"Yes. I know that's not right, but your son has this effect on me. Sometimes, it's hard to tell him no."

I sat there and just listened to everything. I wasn't surprised, because I knew she still loved him. I just wished they just got their shit together and made it official. Things could end badly if they played with each other's hearts.

"I'm not judging you, Serenity. That's y'all business. My only concern is when things go badly, which they will with the games y'all playing, my granddaughter will be in the middle of that mess."

"One minute I want to make it work, and the next I want to try with someone else, who I feel is more worthy of my time. Hakeem had the perfect opportunity to get it right, and he didn't. I played by his rules because I was living under his roof, when he did whatever he wanted to do and expected me to just deal with it. I told you about Rika being in his home around Naomi. I would have never done anything like that."

"I agree. That was wrong on his part, but at the end of the day, you were living with him, and you agreed to his rules. I think you've come a long way. Now, it's time for you to show him that you're a woman and that you're handling things a bit different. However, having doubts in your mind isn't a good thing. If you need to test the waters, do just that, but remember that the grass isn't always greener on the other side."

Serenity was quiet, as if she was in deep thought. Denise started telling me about Rashad and saying I was good for him. She said I didn't take his shit, and he needed someone like me.

We all headed home, and Rashad said he had business to handle with Hakeem. I decided to go home and just relax. It was the first Saturday in a long time that I didn't have plans. The "me time" was much needed.

Serenity

I was sitting with Fallon and doing my progress notes. She looked at me and asked if I had plans for lunch. I laughed because she always wanted greasy food while I tried to stick to a healthy diet. I wasn't on one, but I didn't want my work out to be for nothing. We decided on a hole in the wall joint not too far from the prison. She got wings and fries, and I decided on a ranch chicken wrap.

As we sat and ate our lunch, Fallon asked how things were with Sacar and me. I had really taken a liking to her, so I often shared my dramatic life with her. The smell of the bacon being fried for those who ordered breakfast could be smelled throughout the restaurant.

"I'm actually going to see him after work. I really like him, so I think it's best I be honest with him about my feelings toward Hakeem."

"I don't know if I would do that. Every time you're around Hakeem, Sacar is going to think something is going on between you two."

"I know, but I don't want his feelings to be hurt if things do change between me and Hakeem. I keep thinking that my love for him is only somewhat fitting because I have a child with him."

"So let's picture it this way. If your daughter wasn't here, could you still see yourself loving him?"

I had to think about it for a minute. What we had wasn't ordinary. That was for sure. Everything I did was for Naomi. I stayed with him because of her. If she wasn't around, I probably would have stayed with Shay, even though Hakeem did a lot for me when he didn't have to. He could have put me out and told me to handle shit on my own while he cared for Naomi. He gave me a car to drive, which I was still driving. I had a black card, which was for Naomi, but he always told me to get whatever I needed for myself with it. I don't know another baby daddy who wasn't fucking his baby mama that would do any of that. We went two years without having sex, and he did all of that for me.

"Yes, I do."

"Well, my new found friend, I suggest you figure things out. However, I can't understand why you're allowing him to still be with that girl."

"Honestly, I don't know if he's with her or not. I really don't care. If and when I'm ready for him, trust and know that I'll shut that down."

"I see you, boss lady," she said, smiling.

"So are you looking to date?" I asked.

"Does Hakeem have any friends?" she questioned.

"He does, but he's already taken by my best friend."

"Damn. But when I tell you this, I don't ever want you to repeat it."

I didn't know what the hell she wanted to say, but I got nervous.

"I always have this rule about being professional on my job. It's this prisoner named Faraji that I can't get off my mind. I never saw a man as sexy as him. He just came in last week, and I did his intake screening assessment. He's in because he took a gun charge for his little brother is what I heard. His lawyer worked his magic, and he only got a year. Therefore, you know I told him who I was and what my role would be during his unfortunate stay in prison. I asked him a few questions, and he told me he just wanted to get his time over with so that he could get back to his family. I asked about his family, just trying to get a little personal. He's single, has a younger teenage brother who he cares for, and he has an empire. I know that nigga is a drug lord. I could see it all over his face. I have been dreaming of this man. I'm going to ask if you can take him because I'll fuck around and lose my damn job."

"Fallon, I don't want him if he's looking that sexy that you can't stand to be around him."

We laughed and continued eating.

"It would have been fine if he hadn't asked when the last time was that I'd had some stiff dick and came. I was so caught off guard with that question. I started sweating. Then, he asked why I was so nervous around him. I'm never nervous. I been doing this shit long enough, and here he comes fucking up everything."

"Wow. I mean, you wouldn't fuck him. Where would you fuck him? In his cell block?"

"Don't even play me like that. I wouldn't dare."

We finished our food and headed back to work. I needed to hear more about her and this Faraji character, so I invited her over for drinks at my house for the weekend.

I had just pulled up to Sacar's house. I had to go switch cars with Shay first. He came to the door with no shirt on, and I swear I was hot and bothered. He pulled me into a kiss, and it felt so good to kiss his big juicy lips. Once inside, he pulled me over to his couch and pulled down the shorts I had on. My fake attempt to stop him didn't faze him one bit. He latched on to my lips between my thighs, and he flicked and rotated his tongue. My legs started to shiver as the orgasm formed and released with much force. I couldn't help but let loose and moan out in pleasure. His moans didn't go unnoticed, and I knew he wanted me just as much as I wanted him.

"Damn, you squirted all over Daddy's face. He got up and walked away. I was confused as to why he hadn't continued. Then I thought that maybe he had gone to grab a condom. When he came back, he held a rag and told me I could go in the bathroom if I needed to. I got up and did just that.

Did he not want to fuck after eating my pussy, I thought to myself. I decided to just ask him if something was wrong when I finished washing.

I walked toward the living room where he sat. The surround sound from his system burst with noise from the movie he was playing. I sat down and looked in his eyes.

"What's that look for, ma?" he asked.

"Why didn't you go further?" I asked.

"Because you told me you weren't ready yet. Now if you've changed your mine, we can do some things, baby."

"No. I thought maybe it was for a reason."

"Nah, sexy. I just wanted to taste that pussy."

He grinned, and I laid my head in his lap. I had so much to think about. Was he really who he seemed to be? Alternatively, was he just trying to win me over and eventually change?

"Sacar," I called out to him.

"What up, baby?" he asked.

"We need to talk."

"Okay, my ears open."

"I really like you, and I feel that you like me too, but I want to be honest about something."

"What's that?"

I looked around the house for objects just in case he snapped and tried hurting me.

"Just say it, baby," he requested.

"I haven't been completely honest with you. You asked about my relationship with my baby's father, and I didn't quite tell the truth."

He sat up, and I instantly got nervous. It was too late to turn back. I had already opened the door for the discussion.

"I still love him, and we had some discussion of working things out, but I did tell him somewhat about you and that I really like you," I disclosed.

"Are you fucking him?" he asked.

"No," I fibbed. I just couldn't tell him the truth. I had already felt I told him too much.

"I don't know what to really say, Serenity. A part of me wants to be pissed, but the fact that you're being honest makes me only respect you more as a woman."

"I'm sorry."

"Look, it is what it is. I'm not going to say that I'm not pissed, because I am, but I never had to compete for a woman's heart. If you want to be with him, then do you, but whatever we got ends here. Ain't no going back and forth."

"I wouldn't do that."

"You sure? Because it seems as if you already are. You knew you still loved him, but you're over here getting to know me. I thought you were my girl, but I know better now."

"It's not like that, Sacar."

"Serenity, you can sit here and tell me whatever you want, but at the end of the day, you sat up with that nigga and had a discussion about getting back together. I knew it was something that you kept holding back from me. I just didn't think it was him, after all that shit you told me about the way he treated you. I swear, bitches don't know what the fuck they want from a nigga."

"Excuse you?"

I got up. Now he had pissed me off.

"Look, I have to handle a few things later anyway. You can hit me up when you figure shit out. Since we're being honest, I'm not going to sit around and wait for you to figure it out."

I grabbed my things and jetted for the door. I knew he would be pissed, but basically calling me out of my name was disrespectful. I had dealt with that shit with Hakeem. I wasn't about to start over with someone, only to get treated the same. I was over niggas and their bullshit.

Hakeem

I sat on the other side of the street of Rika's house with Rashad. Shit just wasn't right with her. Some shit I already knew, but I needed more information. We were getting blazed when she ran down the steps of her house, getting into her car. I had one of my soldier's rides so that she wouldn't recognize me. I followed her to her destination. It took about thirty minutes to get where she was going. When she pulled in the driveway and jumped out looking all happy and shit, a nigga came to the door. He looked familiar. I didn't forget a face. I had seen him somewhere before.

"Aye, yo. That's the same nigga Shay was all over that day at the club. Remember when I went over there to shut that shit down while she sat at his table all in his face?"

"Oh yeah, and Serenity was in that hoe ass nigga's face. So this who Rika pregnant by. I knew it wasn't my baby."

"How you know, nigga?" he asked, smirking in a playful manner.

"Unless something was done in my sleep or I got drugged, ain't no way in hell."

We watched as he pulled her in for a kiss. I took a few pictures and pulled off. I had to admit, the house he stayed in was nice, but it didn't have shit on mine. I was pissed that Rika thought she could play me on the baby level. I couldn't wait to rain down on her parade.

"I told you that bitch wasn't right," Rashad voiced.

"Nigga, I told you I'm just playing the hand that I was dealt."

"Call and see if she'll answer."

At first, I was going to, but then I decided not to. There was no point. We headed to the hub so that I could get my car and check that nigga out. I had never seen him before, and with niggas gunning for us, I needed to know who was walking my streets.

"Sup, nigga?" I asked one of my soldiers once we got to the hub. Rashad walked off after speaking. I knew he was trying to get blazed again.

"Shit, still working on finding out who the niggas were that shot at y'all. All we got to go on is that they're from Baltimore. I can hit this lil' cutie up I know. She can look into seeing if anybody recently changed their driver's license from Baltimore with those names, but you know if she does that, she gon' want something from me. Being that I have a girl that's crazy as hell might I add, I ain't trying to go at it like that. I know she will do it for the right price though."

"Say less. Holla at her, and see what you can get. I'll get the money over to you tonight."

If he was any other nigga, I would have told him to just fuck the bitch to get the info we needed. Being that his girl was indeed crazy, I didn't want my boy going through that. I didn't need him stressing. I needed him focused at all times.

My mom called, saying she was bringing Naomi to Serenity. I missed my lil' princess, so I thought I would pop up on them. Serenity had been dodging a nigga and not answering my calls. I had given her ass enough space. I knew she thought I was seeing Rika on some exclusive shit, but it wasn't like that. In the beginning, it was, but once Rashad had told me about her out there being on niggas, I knew it was true. I just needed to see the shit for myself.

After I dropped Rashad off, I headed to Serenity's when Rika's call came through. I smiled because I had been waiting on her ass to call.

"Sup?"

"Hakeem, I been calling your ass all day. Why haven't you been answering?"

"You ain't call me. My phone been on all day."

"I was in the hospital. I had really bad cramps. I thought I was losing our baby."

"Sorry to hear that, but what's this I hear you out here on niggas. You fucking another nigga?" I snapped.

"Hakeem, I would never cheat on you. Why haven't I seen or heard from you? I feel like ever since I told you I was pregnant, you been distant toward me."

Bitch, probably because it ain't mine, but I'll play your game, I thought to myself.

"Look, I just been taking care of shit in the streets. Some shit popped off, and I have to be focused. You know how I get when my attention is on the streets."

"I know, and I just miss you. I just want things to go back how they used to be."

"Look, I have to go. I'll try to come check on you tomorrow, but I have to handle some shit tonight."

"So you're going to be in the streets all night?"

"Something like that."

"You know what? Fuck you and that bitch. I know you're fucking her because you ain't been fucking me. It don't even matter though, because we all gon' be staying together as one big happy mothafucking family!" she yelled.

"Chill out. I'll check you out tomorrow."

She hung up, and a grin spread across my face. I pulled up to Serenity's and got out. I looked around, checking my surroundings and saw one of my soldiers. I laughed because I knew Rashad had put them on me to make sure I was good. *My nigga.*

"Daddy. where are you going to sleep?" Naomi asked.

"Why you all in my business?" I asked her.

"You are my business."

"Nah, I'm not. Until I'm old and grey and can't take care of myself, I'm not your business. You're mine."

"Naomi, time for bed," Serenity called out to her.

"Ugh! Daddy, can I stay up for ten more minutes?" she asked, like that would make much of a difference.

"What did Mommy just say, Naomi?"

She jumped down from my lap and walked slowly to her bedroom. She was already bathed and dressed in her nightgown. Seeing her take her time was the funniest.

"Girl, get your ass in that room, walking slowly. I'm not dealing with your mess tonight. Hurry up."

"I'm thirsty," Naomi told her. I chuckled because she was asking for a butt whooping. She knew her mom didn't play that shit. I guess me being there caused her to act out.

"No. You had juice and water. You're not getting anything else. Go to bed."

"But I wanted some cookies."

"Naomi, take your ass in your room. You know what? I'm about to whoop—"

"Aye, I got it," I said, not wanting to see my baby get her lil' ass whooped. Serenity walked away and sighed. I knew she was frustrated with Naomi.

"Come on. I'll tuck you in, princess."

I tucked Naomi in bed and read her a bedtime story. I even sat there until her spoiled ass dozed off. I walked into the living room to find Serenity on her laptop. She seemed focused on whatever she was doing. When I first got there, I asked if we could talk, and she said yeah. Being that we had an overgrown four-year-old that repeated everything, we wanted to put her to bed first, but of course she wanted to spend time with her daddy.

"Sup, baby," I said.

"You tell me. You the one wanted to talk."

I knew I wasn't tripping. She had a damn attitude.

"I just wanted to see how you been. You haven't returned none of my phone calls or texts."

"Been busy."

"Doing what?"

"Stuff, but if that's all you wanted, you could have just called."

"How, when you don't answer the phone? What's up with you?"

She closed her laptop, and I could see the irritation in her eyes. Something was wrong with her. I had been staying with her for four years. I knew something wasn't right.

"Look, I ain't trying to argue, so if you want me to leave, I will."

"Did I say that?" she asked.

"So what's wrong? You acting all shitty."

"I ended things with ol' boy."

"Oh yeah?"

I smiled and stared at her, even though she wasn't looking at me. I got up and walked over to where she sat. She was in the dining area at the table. I rubbed her shoulders, and she looked up at me.

"What are you doing?" she asked.

"Taking care of my girl."

She tried talking, but I hushed her. I didn't need her telling me she wasn't, because she indeed was. Her shoulders were tense.

"Damn, you're tense as fuck."

I wanted to get her mind off that nigga. It was my time now.

"I know. I keep saying I need to make a trip to the spa, but I haven't gotten to it yet."

When she said that, I knew I had to set up something for us to attend together and enjoy a romantic massage together.

"I think I'm doing a good job. You don't need the spa when you got me."

"You're doing okay, but I like when they get in deep and pound on me."

"I can get in deep and pound on you. My pound game better though. That's for sure."

"I'm talking about a massage," she voiced.

"Shit, me too."

I smirked.

"It does feel good though. Thank you."

"You're welcome," I told her, and I came around to sit in front of her.

"I love you, Serenity. I just want us to be together."

"Are you still with Rika?" she asked.

"The situation with Rika is complicated. I'm not with her, but she doesn't know that we're not together. I'm trying to catch her up in a lie about something, but trust me, it's over."

"Hakeem, that don't even sound believable."

"I know, but just trust me on this. You know it's street re-lated. Otherwise, I would have been dropped that bitch."

She didn't respond. I wanted to fuck her so bad, but I knew she would only think I just wanted to fuck her.

"I'm tired as hell, so I'm going to head home. I will grab Naomi tomorrow from moms, and don't worry. I'll be in my mom's ride.

She gave me a weird look. I thought she was going to say some shit like she didn't want Naomi riding with me at all until the shit in the streets was over and done with.

"You don't want to stay?"

"Do you want me to stay?"

"I mean, your house is a lil' drive. I thought maybe if you're tired, you can sleep here. You can take the couch or sleep on Naomi's floor."

"You know damn well I ain't sleeping on no floor, and the couch would be straight, but I'd rather sleep next to you."

"I umm... I guess."

I walked off toward her room to get a towel and shower. She came in a few minutes later looking at me.

"What's up?"

"Nothing, just watching you do your thing. Make yourself at home."

"Oh, I am. You already know."

She laughed and walked in her closet. I looked at her ass and licked my lips. I had to keep my word. I said to myself that I wasn't going to fuck her. After my shower, I found her sitting on the side of the bed with her hair scarf on, looking at a paper. Her back was facing me. She heard me coming closer, so she turned around.

"Damn! What the fuck?" I asked her. She had on some green facial cream.

"It's to keep my skin from breaking out. You know my skin is sensitive."

"You look like a mothafucking—"

"Hakeem, shut up," she stated, laughing. She hated when I started clowning her ass.

"I'm fucking with you, sexy. You know you're still beautiful, even with that shit on your face."

She stared at my body. The only thing I had on was a towel wrapped around my waist.

"You gon' keep staring or come kiss me?"

"Neither."

"Aight, but can you wash my boxers for me."

She looked at me crazy.

"You know where it's at. Have at it."

"Damn, a nigga can't get his boxers washed?"

"Yeah, just not by me. I have to work in the morning, and I'm tired."

"I got you."

I walked out to wash my undershirt and drawers. I didn't make a habit of washing my clothes. I usually took them to the cleaners, which reminded me that I needed to get my other shit out.

When I got back in the room, she had on some stretch pants and sports bra.

"Where the hell you going?"

"To the living room. I work out every other night for about thirty to forty-five minutes."

"With that green shit on your face?"

"Move," she said, pushing me out the way. I laughed and laid on the bed. After about ten minutes, I decided to check her out while she was working out. When I walked in, she was doing squats. Obviously, it was working because her ass was swollen, but her form was a little off. I walked up behind her and squatted behind her ass as she did her squats.

"Keem, what are you doing?"

"Just trying to help your form. You got it, but keep your shoulders like this, and poke your ass out more. Spread your feet an inch more. Yeah, like that. You got it. Damn!"

My dick instantly rose, and I knew she felt it. I sat on the couch and watched her do her thing for about twenty minutes, which turned into her doing 120 high knees. After she finished, she showered and came to bed. I looked at the clock. If she did that every other day, I knew it had to be hard, especially dealing with Naomi.

"I see you washed that shit off your face."

"I don't sleep with it on."

"So you do that shit every other night? How you managed to do that, especially with Naomi. You been doing that shit since you stayed with me? I never saw you exercise."

"Naomi don't act like that when you're not here. When I tell her to take her ass to bed, she does. You got her spoiled, so she knows when to act up. When I was staying with you, I did it in my room at night and sometimes throughout the day when you weren't there."

"You did a lot of shit I didn't know about when I wasn't there."

She didn't respond. She just turned around and turned her lamp off. I laid there naked, unknown to her. I had my arms behind my head, staring at the wall. It was so much shit I had to handle in the streets, and I still didn't have info on who the niggas were. I prayed to God that he watched over me. Although I didn't live my life according to him, I still had a daughter to raise.

Serenity

I looked over at Hakeem, and he seemed to be in deep thought. Although he always played Superman, I knew he sometimes carried the weight of the world on his shoulders. To hear that someone was out there trying to basically kill him brought fear to my heart. Despite the shit we had been through, I loved and was in love with him. I didn't want anything to happen to him.

"What are you thinking about?" I asked him.

"Go to sleep. You have to be up in less than six hours."

"I'll be fine, but tell me."

"When you broke up with me years ago, was it really because you felt I was controlling?"

"Yes, you treated me like a child. Everything I did, I had to make sure it was cool with you first."

"I'm sorry, baby. I didn't know you really felt that way. I thought it was something else."

"Like what?"

"I don't know. I assumed you left because you wanted to see what else was out there for you. I thought you stayed around because it was convenient for you. Although I played a major part in it because I wasn't letting Naomi go anywhere, I thought you'd eventually leave," he admitted.

"Did you want me to leave?" I asked.

"No. I wanted to ask you for another chance, but I felt you didn't want me. You barely talked to me, and when you did, it was about Naomi. I had mad respect for you though as a mother because you put her first, no matter what. That smart ass mouth she got is because you taught her so much. She doesn't know where to use all of that knowledge."

"You're right about that but thank you. I try my best with her. She's a handful, as you already know."

"Are you ready to try again?"

"I don't want to make the call until whatever you got going on with that bitch is over."

"I got you, ma," he told me.

"Is there something else on your mind?" I questioned.

"Nah, you know I'm always thinking about the streets, but I'm trying to get another hustle going by opening up a business."

"Really? That's awesome, Keem."

"I love when you call me Keem. That means we're on good terms.

"Whatever! I call you both, however it comes out."

I turned toward him, and he was still looking up at the ceiling.

"Why you just staring at a nigga?" he asked.

"I'm just trying to figure out why you're laying like that."

He smirked and told me to go to bed.

"Goodnight, Hakeem."

"It's Hakeem now, huh?"

"I told you whatever comes out."

"Where my goodnight kiss at?" he asked.

At first, I was tempted to say something smart, but I figured what the hell and leaned over to kiss him. He slipped his tongue inside of my mouth, and I tasted a hint of mint. His arms were still behind his head. I couldn't help but rub his chest. My baby daddy's body was sick. He only worked out a little bit, but you would think he stayed in the gym. I rubbed down his chest and stomach. I moved my leg and felt skin contact. He no longer had the towel wrapped around him.

"Hakeem?" I said, pulling away from the kiss.

"Sup?"

"Are you naked?"

"Yeah, why?"

"Boy, you do the most. Goodnight."

I turned around, thinking he would come take it. When he didn't, I turned back around, and his eyes were closed. I wanted him, but I decided to take my lil' horny ass to sleep.

∞∞∞

I woke up to the best pleasure of my life. Hakeem was eating away at my pussy as if it was the last meal he'd ever eat. I spread my legs more, as if I wanted his tongue to reach a place I knew it couldn't. I arched my back as I felt an immense release coming from within me. I came hard before, but at that moment, it was the hardest he'd ever made me come off his head game.

"Oh yes, Keem... I'm cummin'."

When I said that, he spread my legs more and started sucking all of my juices. He surprised me when he started licking my ass crack. That shit did something to me, and I came again.

"Good morning, baby," he told me after sitting up and licking his lips. My juices were everywhere on his face.

"Good morning."

"You better get up and get ready for work, baby."

I did just that in record time. Usually, I dragged around, yelling for Naomi to get up. After I got her up, she would fall back to sleep on the couch. I was out the house twenty minutes earlier than when I usually left. Hakeem stayed behind and slept until he was ready to get up and get his day started. He assured me that his mom would be to get Naomi. It wasn't that I didn't trust him protecting our daughter. I just couldn't take that chance.

I had managed to break two nails while working. I felt so ratchet with my nails looking the way they did. I tried my best to hide them whenever I went to talk with a prisoner. Fallon and I had a meeting with the head liaison worker over the social workers. I thought Fallon had gotten herself into some shit.

"Hello, Serenity," Jeanne said to me as I took a seat in her office.

"Hello."

"Fallon," she said, speaking to her.

"I brought you ladies in to talk about something I noticed. Fallon, you have done great over the years with the prisoners and training Serenity. I know it hasn't been a month yet, but Serenity, I am very impressed with the work you have done so far."

"Well, Fallon is a great mentor. She has shown me the ropes, and I took the lead."

"I know, and that is why I want you to be the social worker coordinator. I know it will take time for you to transition into that role, but I think Fallon can show you how it's done."

I was excited, but I didn't know what that meant for Fallon. Was I taking her position? Was she being fired? I didn't want to lose our friendship over it, but I wasn't going to decline the offer either.

"So what does that mean for Fallon?" I asked. It was no

point in just sitting around wondering.

"Oh yeah, Fallon. We're going to remove you from that role as soon as you train Serenity."

"I don't understand why I'm being fired after all I've done here."

"Fired? We're not firing you. You're going to become the head liaison worker."

"Wait, what?" Fallon asked with a big smile on her face.

"Yes, I am retiring in a few months. When they asked about a replacement, you came in mind, as well as you, Serenity. You two are great at what you do. Fallon, if you accept, this will mean a lot more working hours for you because while you're training Serenity, I have to also train and work with you on a few things."

"Of course I accept. I can't believe this."

The smile on Fallon's face was priceless. I could only imagine mine. Jeanne talked with us about other personal things in her life. She was only sixty-five and in good health, but I understood that she wanted to spend time with family. She wished us a great weekend, and we left.

Fallon and I went to lunch, and she treated. I didn't complain. We both had some celebrating to do.

"If we make plans, are you going to come this time?" I asked her.

"Yes, I told you that my mom wanted me to come visit her for the weekend, but I think I have something going on this weekend as well. I'll check my calendar. My friend is getting married, and she wants to announce it this weekend. She's pregnant."

"Wow! That's a lot to celebrate."

"It is. I haven't really talked with her in some time, because she's always with him, but I can't blame her. He is fine. I don't even know her fiancé's name or anything, but I'll meet him."

"Well, let me know when you're free because we have to celebrate together, and I want you to meet my best friend. And guess what?"

"What?" she said, biting into her sandwich?

"Hakeem and I are making progress. I'm not going to say we're in a relationship just yet. We both have baggage to get rid of."

"Aww, you looked so happy saying that. I really hope it works out for you two."

"Anyway, heifer, I see that you didn't switch Faraji off to me."

"Girl, I thought about it, but I wanted to see him again. He wasn't so talkative today though. He seemed down, but I don't know."

"Interesting."

"Oh, shut up, but I need to get over my crush for this man. He's in prison for crying out loud."

"I can see the news headline now. Faraji and Fallon, a cell block love."

"Bitch, I mean, girl shut up," she said, cracking up laughing.

"Let's go, before we're late."

After work, I called Hakeem and told him the good news.

"Damn, that's what's up, baby. I'm so proud of you. Let me take you to dinner to celebrate."

"Aww, you don't have to do that, Keem."

"I know I don't, but I want to. Go home and get dressed. I'll call mama and let her know that we'll be to get Naomi a little later. I'm glad I got my shit re-twisted today," he said.

I looked at the clock and wondered if I had time to get my nails fixed. I figured I did, so I jumped off the exit to the nail salon. I called Shay on the way there and told her the good news as well. She asked where I was, and I told her I was on my way to the nail salon. She wanted to meet there too because she had broken a nail.

Shay sat next to me as the tech fixed our nails. I was so happy and ready to get home and get dressed. It was Friday, so I wanted to celebrate all night with Hakeem and indulge in some adult activities.

"I'm so proud of you, boo. Look at you. I knew God favored you," Shay said.

"Aww, thanks, boo. Oh, and what happened to your nail?"

"Girl, Rashad's ass got a little rough the other day."

"I should have known."

"Whatever! It's only one. You got two that are broken, so Hakeem must have been a little rougher with you."

"Bitch, first off, this happened at work."

"Yeah, so you say."

She got up and headed to the register to pay. I looked up and saw Rika walking in. I laughed to myself because out of all the nail shops, she had to stop in the same one as me. Shay turned around to look at me, and I knew she wanted to say something, but I gave her that look. Rika looked up and locked eyes with me. She seemed shocked. Then, a weird grin spread across her face. After my nails dried, I got up to pay.

"Well, if it isn't Serenity. What you doing? Spending more of my man's money, huh?"

"Bitch, move before I black both eyes this time."

Shay was now by my side.

"Oh, please do it so that I can press charges on you. This

time, you will go to jail for hitting a pregnant woman."

I looked down and noticed a small bulge, but what I couldn't understand was why she said it as if I was supposed to be hurt by it.

"Yes, Naomi will have a brother or sister. I prefer a boy so that I can name him after his father."

Shay and I both laughed. I stood toe to toe with Rika and looked into her eyes.

"I hope like hell you didn't tell Hakeem you were pregnant by him."

"Bitch, why wouldn't I tell my man we're having a baby? And he's excited. He can't wait to start a family."

"You're a dead bitch. Hakeem can't have any more kids. That nigga got a vasectomy years ago. I know because I put ice on his dick for four weeks straight."

Her eyes bulked, and her mouth dropped. I smiled because she was one evil conniving bitch. Now I knew what Hakeem meant when he said he was trying to catch her in a lie.

"Here your mouth go, hoe. It was on the floor," I said, attempting to pick it up for her.

"Thought you might've caught a lick," Shay sang out. I couldn't help but to fall over laughing. We left that bitch in the nail shop looking bothered while we walked out unbothered, but I had to admit that I had a bone to pick with Hakeem.

"That shit was so funny. She thought she had your ass with that one too. Bitch thought she was about to end your world today with that news," Shay said, laughing.

"Hakeem gon' kill that hoe. Let me get home and see what his ass has to say about this shit."

We both got inside our separate cars and drove home. Once I got in, I showered and got dressed. It wasn't long before Hakeem came walking in the door, asking if I was I ready. He looked very handsome with his button up and slacks on. My man knew how to dress. That was for sure. Evening was approaching, but it was still very hot out. I decided on a nice fitted dress.

"You ain't ready yet, my queen?"

"I am just putting on my eye shadow."

"Nah, you don't need that shit. You're already beautiful, ma."

I smiled, but I still applied the shadow. We were walking out the door, and Hakeem grabbed my ass.

"Can you keep your hands to yourself?"

"Not today. I did that last night, and it was hard as hell."

"So you slept next to me naked just to keep your hands to yourself?"

"Yep. I didn't want you to think that all I wanted was sex from you."

"Aww, babe," I said, hugging him around his neck. I pecked his lips and walked away so that he could shut and lock the door. In the car, I wanted to ask him about Rika, but I waited until we got to wherever we were going.

We pulled up to the restaurant, and I was looking down at my phone. When I looked up, I gasped.

"Hakeem, oh my God! When did it open?" I asked. His mom's restaurant was in full swing. I didn't even know she was open yet.

"It's not, but she said I could take you to dinner here tonight since her chef is here preparing meals. It's just for her workers. They're doing a practice run basically, but they wanted to serve us and show off their skills."

"Oh my God. Let's go in."

I was out the car before he could even open the door for me. The front entrance was nothing but VIP status. The red carpet leading to the door was most definitely Denise's taste. The gold doors were shining. I felt like a celebrity walking in. We were greeted in a friendly and professional manner. I looked around and felt the sense of an upscale expensive restaurant. You knew the food would be delicious. She named it Vi-Cho's, and the name even sounded great.

We were seated and asked for our drink orders. Hakeem ordered champagne. Knowing I wasn't twenty-one yet made me nervous.

"It's cool, ma. I got you."

"Keem, everything looks so great. Coli knows exactly what your mom likes."

"He does. I must say that he's a great man. He's been working on this place for months. He put his blood and sweat into bringing this place alive."

"Look at it, the set up. Wow! I can't wait to tell her everything was great."

Hakeem smiled and grabbed my hands.

"That smile and that phone call I got today from you telling me about your new role at work... that's what makes me happy is seeing you happy. I love you, Serenity, and I hope you know that."

"I do, and I was happy that I could share that with you."

We ate, and I took a million pictures of the place. I had to show Shay. While we ate, I looked up at Hakeem. I needed to know something, and I couldn't wait any longer to ask him.

"Hakeem, I don't want to ruin our dinner, but I have to ask you something."

He put his fork down and gave me his undivided attention.

"I'm listening."

"Have you ever had sex with Rika without a condom?"

"Hell nah!" he yelled.

"Hakeem," I said, hoping he wouldn't get so loud.

"My fault, but why you asked that?"

"Shay and I saw her at the nail shop. She told me she was pregnant by you."

"That bitch crazy as hell. That's why I told you that whatever I'm doing with her is street related. Something ain't right about her and whoever this nigga is that she's fucking with, but you know I don't like talking about that shit with you."

"I know. Rika said Naomi was going to have a little sister or brother, but she wanted a boy to name him after you."

"I wish that bitch would name that fucker after me. It's crazy because if you hadn't known that shit about me, you would have probably believed her."

"I probably would have, and I can see now that bitches are truly devious."

Rika

I sat Indian style on Moni's bed. I was afraid that if I stepped foot out of this house, Hakeem would kill me. He knew all this time that the baby wasn't his, and he let me believe I had him fooled. I had no choice but to tell Moni' it was his now.

"Baby, what's wrong?" Moni asked. The tears came rolling down my face.

"I'm pregnant."

"Pregnant?"

"Yes."

"Okay. It's okay, baby. Don't cry about it. We been fucking like rabbits, so it was going to happen. I got you. Don't even worry about that."

"I have to tell you something else."

"Okay, talk."

"I was dating this guy named Hakeem, and he's upset that I'm pregnant by someone else. He said he was going to kill me."

"Hakeem? You know where that nigga stay?"

I didn't know if I should tell him or not. I wanted to be sure Hakeem was indeed mad at me. He'd had plenty of opportunities to get at me, but he didn't.

"Nah, I never been to his house," I lied.

"You think you could find out?"

"Yeah, but why?"

"I mean, a nigga fucking threatening my girl and my un-born child. He has to be dealt with."

"I will get the information for you."

He kissed me, and I smiled. If Hakeem wanted his life, he had to now play by my rules. Serenity had another thing coming if she thought I was going to let her get away with embarrassing me in front of her friend.

Shayla

Serenity begged me to come out with her and her co-worker, Fallon. She knew I didn't like fucking with new people, especially females. Being that they were celebrating their promotions, I decided to go. We were not really feeling the club thing, so we decided on dinner.

"So Fallon, how old are you?" I asked.

"I'm twenty-four, and you?"

"I'm twenty-three."

"Okay, so you're older than the baby over here?"

She pointed at Serenity, and we laughed.

"Yes, she's the youngster in the click."

We all chatted, and I really got to know Fallon. She was down to earth and funny as well. Serenity asked her about her friend's engagement thing, and she said it was cancelled.

"I called her up to get the address the day before, and she said it was cancelled. They were having complications with the baby or something. I don't know. Honestly, I think that her and this guy's relationship doesn't even exist. She's been my friend for years, so I know she sometimes make up stories about her life to try to compete with mine. I told her once before that she didn't have to do that. I'm trying to remain friends with her, but something tells me we will eventually go our separate ways."

I looked at Fallon and thought she was a very pretty girl. She could most definitely roll with us more often.

"So that's it. Did she give you an update on if they were going to reschedule everything?" Serenity asked.

"Nope, I'm over it. I think she's lying, but all I can do is be a supportive friend. When she calls, I'll be there."

They told me stories about their job and the shit they dealt with on a daily basis. After dinner, we decided to go to little spot where people drink and did karaoke. I laughed because the last time we went, Serenity sang the whole Destiny's Child album. I laughed so hard that I was falling out of my chair with all the hollering she was doing.

"Serenity, did y'all make it official yet?" I asked.

"Yes, bitch. It's official. You know that's been Daddy."

"I know, that's why you ain't give that pussy up. You know what it was."

"Oh my God. Shut up."

"I'm just saying. Hakeem wasn't having that shit. He kept spitting in my ear about being with you. That's why we started brainwashing you about being with him."

"Bitch, you didn't brainwash shit. I'm with him because I love him."

"Okay, watch. When I snap my finger, tomorrow you're going to hate each other."

"You do know if that comes true, I'm coming after you, right?"

"I'm playing, man, but I'm so happy that y'all worked it out. You know how hard it was being mad at my brother? He never questioned me though about being his friend first. He knew I would take your side over his."

"Yes, he clearly knew," she said.

"What you over there thinking about?" Serenity asked Fallon.

"Faraji, girl. He's so damn fine. I can't believe I'm even saying that."

They put me up on game about the Faraji guy. I laughed so hard, but I told her what was up.

"Girl, if you think he's what you say he is, you better get on that. You have the power to get in his head and fuck with him. Use your profession to bag that nigga."

They laughed, but I was serious.

"Girl, Shay is crazy. You have to excuse her."

"No, I like her style. I may have to do what she says," Fallon agreed.

"Lord, I can't have the both of you acting crazy."

Serenity laughed.

"I'm glad I came out. Fallon, you're cool peeps. I usually don't fuck with newcomers, but I enjoyed your company. Now I hate to do this, but my man just texted me saying he's at home waiting on me, so your girl gotta bounce."

"Really, Shay? The dick can wait."

"Oh, the dick can wait, but this kitty down here can't."

They laughed so hard, but I was dead serious.

"Call me tomorrow, not too early though. Congratulations to the both of you ladies, and I hope you enjoy the rest of the night. Serenity, don't stay out too late, because I don't want Hakeem calling and asking where your ass at while Rashad sucking on me."

"Bitch, bye," Serenity said. They walked me out to the car and left as well. I wasn't trying to ruin their fun, but Daddy had called.

After making love to Rashad, he told me he loved me over

and over. I laughed because he was starting to sound like a broken record.

"Move in with me, ma."

"Move in with you?"

"Yes, we're either here together or at my house. I think we should be in one spot to make it our own."

"That's cool, but you're so far from my job, and it's so convenient living here. I'm close by everyone and everything."

"So you're saying no?"

"I didn't say no. I'm telling you what I'm saying."

"Yeah and it sounds like no to me."

"Rashad, you don't get what I'm saying."

"I get it, Shay, loud and clear."

He got up and walked into the bathroom. I shook my head because I did love him, but I was used to my space and having my own. Rashad came from the bathroom and just stared at me. I gave him the "aww" look because it wasn't my intention to hurt his feelings.

"Are you with a nigga out of convenience?"

"Convenience of what, Rashad?"

"You know what I'm talking about. You basically call me when you want to, and I can't always get a hold to you. Like tonight, I called. You came because you wanted it, but in two or three days, you'll be telling me you're chilling and don't feel like doing anything. It's basically your way of saying you don't want to be bothered."

"Baby, it's not like that. Yes, I love my space, but it's not anything against you. I love being with you. I just think we need to think about moving in with each other. What's wrong with that?"

He looked at me and walked over to the bed. He got under

the covers and laid down. I stood there wondering what other choice I had. I didn't like lying, so I told him the truth, and he took it the wrong way.

Hakeem

I let Serenity sleep in while I took Naomi and my mom shopping at the mall. I grabbed Serenity a few things as always. My mom was happy that we were together. I had to admit that our love started out as convenient, but it is what it is. We fit together, and I loved her and my daughter more than anything.

"Y'all ready to go?" I asked my mom and Naomi.

"Yes, Daddy. My legs hurt," Naomi whined. I laughed because I had a dozen bags in my hands. I couldn't pick her up.

After getting everything inside of the Bentley, we headed to get some food. I was beyond hungry. It was about eighty degrees outside, and I needed food and something to drink before I passed out.

"Hey, that little hot dog stand at Satan Park had good dogs there. Naomi can eat and play, and we can talk."

"Aight, that's cool."

I shot Serenity a text, telling her that my mom, and I were taking Naomi to the park and to get hot dogs. She told us to enjoy ourselves and that she would be at Shay's. Once we made it to the park, I got out and spotted the hot dog stand. There was a line, so mom and I sat at the bench to watch Naomi play until the line went down.

"Son, are you really ready for a committed relationship?"

"Yes ma'am."

"I'm serious. Serenity has a lot going for herself. Don't ruin her life. She doesn't need you to hold her hand anymore. She has it and can now carry Naomi on her own. If you mess over her, she's going to leave you, and it will be for good. You want to keep talking about you're the man. Well, you'll be a single man. I don't want them lil' heifers calling my house anymore, nor do I want others thinking you're going to cheat. Don't cheat her of love when she deserves all of it."

"I know, ma, and I ended whatever I had going on with those chicks. I'm for Serenity and Naomi, and that's real. I love her and plan to someday give her my last name."

"I wish you could give me more grandbabies," she said.

"Ain't happening, ma."

"Do you know it can be reversed?"

"That shit hurt so fucking bad. I had Serenity walking around with an ice bag trying to relieve the pain," I told her, looking at Naomi about to push someone down the slide. She knew better than to do something like that.

I barked at her, and she looked sad. That spoiled shit had to stop. My mom went to place our orders, and I called Naomi over to me. She took her precious time walking, and I was growing impatient.

"Yes, Daddy?"

"You know better than to push someone down a slide, better yet, putting your hands on them. Don't let me see you doing that again, okay?"

"Okay, Daddy."

I hugged and kissed her and looked up. There was a man standing in front of us. I had to think about who he was and where I had seen him. Then, it clicked. He was at the club that day with that one nigga Rika was fucking with.

"Hello, Naomi. You're looking pretty today, just like your beautiful mom. Make sure you tell her I said hi."

"Nigga, is you stupid? Don't ever speak to my daughter."

"If I was you, I would play it cool. I just wanted to come introduce myself. My name is Sacar. Yes, I'm the one that was looking for you, and I'm the one that shot at you and your boy. I wasn't trying to kill you though. I just needed to get your attention. I was sure you would have found me by now, but you didn't, which makes what I'm about to say so much easier. I want your territory, and I want you to work for me. My resources and power are far more than yours."

"You must be smoking crack. Ain't no way in hell I'll work for you. And the territory? You will never get that. Take your ass back to Baltimore while you're living because otherwise, it'll be in a body bag."

I hated saying all that shit in front of my daughter, but I was heated. That nigga knew who the fuck my daughter was and probably much more. I reached around to feel for my gun when he stopped me.

"Aye, that isn't necessary. I would never kill my girl's baby daddy in front of her child."

When he said that, the expression on my face changed. I was seeing red. I felt cold. I could barely move.

"Yes, Serenity and I have been dating. You were the nigga in the club staring us down the whole night. I didn't know then that you were her baby's father, but it doesn't matter much now. I'll see you around. Since you didn't accept my offer, I have to take it, and you're now considered the enemy."

He walked away, and I wished that Naomi wasn't with me. I wanted to kill him, which was my number one rule in the game... to never let the enemy get away.

I was seeing blood. I dropped my mom and Naomi off to her place because I had to find Serenity. Rika spending the night wasn't shit on her letting that nigga meet my fucking daughter. He called my child out by her name and knew who she was.

I ran into Shay's house. The door was locked, but I kicked that sucker down. Her eyes got big, and she asked what was wrong with me. I asked where Serenity was, and she said in the bathroom. As soon as I got to the door, Serenity was coming out.

"Hakeem, what's wrong?" she asked. I grabbed her up against the bathroom door. Shay started screaming for me to let her go.

"You let that motherfucker see my daughter?" I yelled.

"Hakeem, what are you talking about!"

"Sacar! I saw him in the park not too long ago. He walked over to me, and my fucking daughter and called her out by name," I roared.

"Let me explain, Hakeem."

"You let that nigga see my fucking child?" I yelled.

"Hakeem, please! You're hurting me," she said as my hands went around her neck.

"Did you?"

"Yes. I'm sorry."

To be Continued....

Note From

TNesha Sims

Thank you for reading this new series, *Hakeem & Serenity: Convenient Love of A Boss*. I hope you enjoyed your read. I want to thank you all for being supportive throughout this series. Part two and three is already available. **Please leave a review**. Also, I still have other great reads that you can check out. Also, check out my author page where I drop sneak peeks and much more. Keep rocking with your girl! Peace and love!!

To connect with the writer:

Facebook: @Author TNesha Sims

IG: @authortneshasims

Amazon: amazon.com/author/tneshasims

Email: Sensationpen@gmail.com

Author
T'Nesha Sims
Pen Sensation

Made in United States
North Haven, CT
23 March 2022

17454630R00114